Jungle Mis...

# Legend of the Wapa

A NOVEL BY ERNIE BOWMAN

For Natalie:

*You are usually my first reader, and therefore subjected
to the worst of my drafts.
Amazingly, you continue to read them anyway.
Your selflessness and godliness inspire me every day.*

"This book will thrill the hearts of those who like a good fictional story, but it also will inspire them toward more support and participation in the real life adventure of world missions."

**Dr. Harry L. Reeder, III,** Sr. Pastor, Briarwood Presbyterian Church

"I am a missionary today because a storyteller captured my imagination and made me think, *Hey, maybe I could be a missionary too!* Ernie is a missions-motivating storyteller for a new generation. His book is full of rich details of the realities of modern missionary life, and it's chock-full of 'me too!' moments. He portrays the everyday realities of missionary life in least-reached places. This humorous, engaging story will lead readers to consider their role in reaching the world with the gospel message."

**Elizabeth McAdams,** Student Ministries/Camp Missionary

"The next generation of missionaries are right now in their formative years. The books they read and the stories that they hear from missionaries will bend their hearts to the mission fields of the world. *Legend of the Wapa* is one of the books that should be on the book shelf of those who are the potential missionaries of tomorrow."

**Paul Seger,** General Director, Biblical Ministries Worldwide

"A good teacher knows that a story will stick with his students longer than a straight lecture. Much longer— maybe even a lifetime. Ernie Bowman is a good teacher, and *Legend of the Wapa* is a good story. It's an adventure story, a mystery story, and you might even say the story is a romance; after all, what is more powerful than love—love, not of self, but love of a Being who has revealed Himself as worthy of worship, or love of neighbor that moves us to venture across cultural lines, or the love of Christ that compels us to live our one brief life for something bigger than ourselves.

*Legend of the Wapa* is a thoughtful telling of how zeal builds in Ian Allen's life, and how he, an ordinary American, is willing to go and intertwine his life with the lives of people in a small village in the jungle. Ian and his wife become rich in ways that matter, and find themselves in the middle of a once-in-a-lifetime event that only the elders in the tribe have heard about. You'll find yourself turning pages to solve the mystery and finish the adventure, but you might also be surprised that Ian's life appeals to something deep inside of you, something that you've maybe never fully identified, but is as real as the water in the ocean."

**Paul Gardner,** Director, Camp Barakel

"I started reading and couldn't put the book down...a masterful job!

As one who seldom reads fiction, I was both entertained and challenged by Ernie's Bowman's *Legend of the Wapa*. Written in an engaging style, the story drew me in, and I read with anticipation. Although fiction, Brother Bowman's story is seasoned with real-life missionary experience, preparation, and ministry.

*Legend of the Wapa* will be formative for adults and children alike. I recommend this as an excellent read-aloud to children and grandchildren. I'm sure you'll find yourself, along with me, moved to reflection, laughter, and tears. I started reading and couldn't put the book down...a masterful job. I look forward to the next in the series—may the Lord use this for his glory!"

**Dr. Marty Marriott,** President, Maranatha Baptist University

Visit **CruciformPress.com**

for more Cruciform Fiction books
as well as

*Bible Studies for Women*
*by Keri Folmar*

and more than sixty Christian-living titles
from top authors such as

**John Piper**
**Tim Challies**
**Jerry Bridges**

and many more

Legend of the Wapa

Print / PDF ISBN: 978-1-949253-09-2
Mobipocket ISBN: 978-1-949253-10-8
ePub ISBN: 978-1-949253-11-5

Published by Cruciform Press, Minneapolis, Minnesota. Copyright © 2019 by Ernie Bowman

## Chapter 1

The curtains are drawn tight across the window and just a bit of light filters around the edges to catch the side of my face. My eyes crack open and I am momentarily confused. It takes me a second to remember where I am, but I don't panic. This happens often enough that I'm used to it.

I take in the not-so-familiar sight of the new gray-blue curtains on the windows and marvel at how good of a job they do at keeping the sunlight at bay. Sunrise comes early here and I have never been a morning person. Because of that I didn't object when my wife wanted to splurge on some new curtains. The old ones looked okay, but they did a lousy job of keeping my bedroom dark in the morning. I'm up early for work every day during the week, so when the weekend gets here I want to sleep in. My neighbors think I'm nuts and they can't seem to figure out why I don't want to get up at the crack of dawn every day like they do. Literally. They are up at dawn, every day, without fail. Weekends included. Why? That's just what they do. They cook breakfast and then most of them head outside to work in their gardens.

"That is what we have always done," they say, as if it were the most natural thing in the world. "Work in the light, sleep in the dark."

I've thought about trying to explain the terms "weekend" and "night owl" to them, but whatever—to each his own, right? Anyway, enough musing about my sleep habits. There are things that need to be done right away today if the rest of the day is going to go as planned. And I desperately want the rest of the day to go as planned.

I swing my legs out of bed and head across the bedroom and out to the kitchen. I can hear my wife singing softly in the shower as I begin the familiar routine of starting the day. I glance out the front window to make sure no one moved my motorcycle during the night, then head like a zombie for the coffee pot. I heard one time that there are actually people in the world who drink decaf coffee. For what purpose, I have no idea. Clearly those people don't understand coffee and should not be trusted.

Once the coffee pot is gurgling its way toward a steaming pot of life-giving, caffeinated goodness, I turn my attention to this morning's special preparations. This is no ordinary day of the week. It's Sunday.

Sundays mean two things, each of them special to me in their own way. First of all, and most important, it's Church Day. It's the one day of the week where nearly every Christian in town gets together. We've been living different lives all week, but each Sunday we put those individual lives on hold for a few hours. Coming together as one, we give our attention and our worship to the Lord.

That comes first.

But after church, it's also Game Day.

It's the one day of the week where I kick back, pig out, and indulge in that quintessential American pastime: watching football. Football has been my favorite sport ever since I was a kid. I can still remember the first time I saw Barry Sanders dance his way across the field for the Detroit Lions. No one could touch him. He twisted grown men into knots, leaving them grabbing at air. I wanted to do that. Every kid in Detroit did, I'm sure of it. Or, at least I think they did. I actually have no idea because I'm not from Detroit. I'm from Lapeer, a small town just a few miles down the freeway from Flint. No one has ever heard of Lapeer, but everyone in the country seems to have heard about Flint. At least the water anyway. I have no idea what "Lapeer" actually means, but we used to say it's French for "the back of beyond." I could tell you stories of growing up with miles of woods and fields to play in, wishing like crazy we had cable TV, or even air conditioning, but that will have to wait for another time. Like I said, I've got stuff to do.

I start the warm water at the tap and when it's hot I dump the right amount into a bowl and add the yeast. Sugar and salt go in next and the whole thing gets stirred and set aside for a few minutes. This is the other thing that makes Sundays so great: pizza. I have no idea where she learned how to make pizza, because her step-mom is a terrible cook, but my wife makes the best pizza in this entire country. Hands down, no contest. And there is nothing in the world that can make a guy feel more American than spending a Sunday afternoon eating pizza and watching football, which is exactly what I intend to do today. It's what I did last Sunday, the Sunday before that, and, Lord willing, next Sunday too. It probably seems like a little thing to anyone else, but to me it's an important ritual.

It helps me keep my sanity and feel connected to back home, especially when I think about how different and dangerous things can be here. Not that I'm expecting a whole lot of excitement today, but you just never know.

With the yeast beginning to foam in the mixing bowl, I take a couple glass bottles of Coke from the cupboard and put them in the back of the fridge. As always I'm careful to open the door quickly, get the Coke inside, and shut the door as quick as I can. Time elapsed: less than two seconds. Minimizing the amount of cold air that escapes is critical. Our fridge is old and doesn't work that well, so I have to do this if I want the Cokes to be the right temperature for game time—just short of freezing, but only barely.

The initial preparations are done and I can no longer hear the water running in the bathroom. That means my wife is out of the shower and it's my turn. I head in that direction, realizing as I go that I have managed to gulp down three cups of coffee already this morning. If I had known then what was lying in wait for me over the next few days, I would have made an extra pot and taken the time to savor it more. Sometimes hindsight really is 20/20.

Having no clue what's coming, I briefly consider how much coffee is too much, before remembering there's no such thing.

By the time I get out of the shower, get dressed, and finish checking the morning's email, my wife is dressed and ready to go. She takes less time to get ready in the morning than most of the men I know from back home, and I silently thank God for her again. A rare combination of beautiful and low-maintenance, she truly is one-of-a-kind. She is in the kitchen adding the finishing touches to the pizza dough as I come through the door and give her a kiss on the cheek.

"How'd you sleep last night?" She asks with genuine interest, taking a sip of coffee.

"Long and well," I reply, knowing full well what's coming next.

"I'll say. I tried to wake you up when I left the bed this morning, but you barely stirred. I guess those curtains are worth the extra we paid for them after all?"

Her smile gives her away and I know she's just messing with me. I'm normally pretty tight-fisted when it comes to spending money, and she knows the premium we paid for those curtains hurt my heart a little bit.

"Worth every penny," I concede. "Come on, we'll be late for church if we don't leave now. Is the dough done?"

"Of course it's done. It's Sunday, isn't it? And we don't need to rush—it's not like they'll start without you."

We head out the door together, my wife pausing to place the dough bowl in the corner of the porch. From there it will rise slowly while we're gone, as the morning heats up. We live just south of the church, close enough to walk there, which is exactly what we've done every week since we moved here. We get to church on time, find our seats in the front, and begin the familiar and comfortable routine of the Sunday-morning church service.

It's probably almost exactly like the service at your church last Sunday: opening prayer, a chorus, announcements, another song, an offering, more singing, Scripture reading, and a sermon from a Bible passage. The sermon goes longer than usual but I'm not worried about missing the kickoff, because the game I'll be watching has been taped. That's a blessing the 15-year-old me would have been insanely jealous of.

I can remember as a kid that my parents would stay after church talking, and talking, and talking. Always the endless talking. They acted as if they had no clue there was a game we were missing. And I would keep checking the time over and over again, knowing that the longer they talked, the more football I would miss. Now, with the advent of modern technology, I don't even worry about it anymore.

So we take our time chatting with friends after church. We hear about how so-and-so's niece just took her first steps. We smile to mask the disappointment at not having kids of our own. We are genuinely happy for them, but it still hurts. We finally close up the doors and head for home, retracing the familiar steps up the path.

Ninety minutes later the pizza is hot and the Cokes are cold. I press play on the remote control and kick back on the couch. My wife sits down next to me and I wonder again: *How many guys have a woman who willingly watches football with them? No wonder I love her so much.*

I cheer and chow my way through the game. I thank God for technology as I fast forward through the commercials. I'll admit the beer commercials are sometimes funny, but the prescription drug commercials? Not so much. I slow it down to listen to the commentary at halftime. As the post-game show wraps up I reflect for just a second on how very routine my afternoon was. The pizza was delicious. The Lions lost. And I am still the luckiest guy on earth. I know it's probably not right how much I like football, but I have come to accept my own idiosyncrasies in that way. My neighbors, however, have not. They can't understand why I love the game so much. This conversation from church is typical...

A neighbor of mine, Bigfoot (not his real name, but that's what we all call him), came up to me one day as I was walking by his house.

"Headed home to watch the game?" he asked.

"Of course," I told him. "It's Sunday, isn't it?"

"It is, yes. But it is such a violent game; it seems so savage and cruel. The people who play must have very primitive minds, to find it fun. Besides, aren't games for children?"

"Many of them are, Bigfoot, you're right. Maybe that's why I like this one so much. It keeps me young at heart."

(I know, I know, that's a pretty thin argument, but I wasn't sure what else to tell him. We'd had this same conversation at least five times.)

"Well, I hope your friends win. You seem to love them very much."

I was still trying to figure out if I should be insulted by his cryptic reply when he clapped me on the shoulder and walked away. No doubt he spent the afternoon at home resting, just as soon as his garden was weeded perfectly. In that regard we're not that much different after all.

With Bigfoot still on my mind, I stand up from the couch and stretch, clicking off the TV in the process. As I turn around I can see some other neighbors out front. They have their faces pressed against the window, hands cupped to fight the glare, peering into my living room. I wave and walk toward the front of the house. They back up two steps as I come out the door.

"Hello, Mister Neighbor!" Henry calls out as I close the door. "Did your team do the killing today?"

His smile stretches from ear-to-ear as he says it, because he knows no one was being killed on my TV. He still has no idea what is actually happening on the football field, but he knows enough to give me a hard time about it. Most of the people around here good-naturedly call football The Killing Game. The first time they saw it they said it looked like everyone was trying to catch and kill the man holding the funny shaped fruit. Others said it looked like a group of children trying to catch and kill a small bird.

"No, Henry, not today," I reply with a smile of my own, as I clasp his lower arm in greeting. This kind of handshake would be foreign to my friends back home, but here it is the social norm. Grasping another man by the wrist and offering your own wrist is a way of demonstrating trust. It shows you have nothing up your sleeve. Even though no one here has sleeves.

"Too bad," Henry replies, his smile never dimming. "You would think a lion could kill whatever it wanted. Yours is a strange world, my friend."

"Yes it is, Henry, yes it is."

I release his wrist and he transfers his fishing spear back to the right hand as he and his group continue down the path. They are headed south past the airstrip to the river, in search of supper for their families. I'll join them as soon as I can.

Perhaps at this point I should introduce myself properly.

In case you haven't guessed by now, I am not your average football fan. I love football; I love America; I love pizza, Coke, and my wife Rachael (though not necessarily in that order). In some ways this has been a typical American Sunday, complete with church, pizza, and football. But it hasn't taken place in America.

I live in Venezuela.

At least I think I do. I've been told by some visiting groups that my house actually sits on the border of Venezuela and Brazil, but don't tell that to my neighbors. Their village may straddle that border, but when you try and talk to them about countries and borders they just get confused.

"No," they will reply. "This is our land. Venezuela is not one of our ancestors. This has always been our land. We do not know this man Venezuela."

What's funny is how weird that sounds when you say it out loud, but also how right it sounds when you think about it. Anyway, my house is apparently situated directly on the border, but you would never know it by looking around. From where we sit on the front porch the jungle of Venezuela in the front yard looks exactly the same as the jungle of Brazil in the backyard.

But I digress. Back to introductions.

My name is Ian Allen and I am a jungle missionary, although the people who write the pamphlets and other such things back home in the States don't like it when I say it that way. I'm supposed to say "tribal missionary." Apparently saying "jungle" will make kids these days not want to be missionaries. Personally, I don't really get that. For one, I love how it sounds to say "jungle missionary." And, if you ask me, what better way to make young people want to do something than to make it sound like Indiana Jones works in the cubicle next to you. Though we don't have cubicles in the jungle, of course. Which, come to think of it, is one of the many reasons why I love working here.

And besides, the bottom-line truth is that I live and work in the jungle. My wife Rachael and I have been here for almost two years now. We arrived here with a team of six people—two couples and two single guys. We were the initial group of adventurous jungle missionaries (see how cool that sounds?) trying to bring the good news of Jesus and the message of the gospel here for the first time in history.

"Here" is officially named Indigenous Outpost 139 by the Venezuelan government, although their maps actually have it located about 12 miles further north than it actually is. To the Kilo people who live here, it's simply called Bahwee.

Home.

It is the only place most of them have ever known. There are no cities or even towns anywhere close by, and only a few other tribes within walking distance—as long as you measure walking distance in terms of days and not minutes. Even going by river, the fastest form of transportation they have here can take several days of paddling downstream before you come to the nearest cluster of "civilized" humanity.

So if something goes wrong, we are very much on our own and have to deal with it ourselves.

## Chapter 2

At this point you're probably wondering why an American boy from Michigan would choose to live and work in the jungle. It's a legit question, but you have to know—the Kilo people are not savages. They are not cannibals or devil worshipers or anything like that. I'm supposed to call them "tribal people" (again, the office types back home have chosen the vocabulary), but I mostly just call them friends.

I know, I know. That sounds cheesy enough to make broccoli edible, but it's true. Over the course of the last two years many of the Kilo have become my friends and I can't think of any better way to describe them in my letters to home. "Tribal people" sounds too formal. "Natives" always make people think of "naked." And "Indigenous People Group" is too big of a mouthful. "Friend" or "neighbor" typically works well.

Right, you say, but what am I doing here? The short answer is that we're translating the Bible. The goal of our mission outpost is to complete a Kilo language translation of the Bible. Once that's done we can teach them about Jesus directly from God's Word and help them build a self-perpetuating church community of their own. If I wanted to sound impressive (an occasionally useful skill back home on the fundraising trail), I would tell you that our mission team is "engaged in a strategic, long-range, evangelistic church-building and outreach plan with the goal of spreading the gospel of grace to the indigenous tribal people groups of west-central Venezuela and Brazil." Talk about a mouthful! That's why I typically just say we're here to translate the Bible.

Nice plan, right? Yeah, we thought so, otherwise we wouldn't be here. Consider this though—the Kilo have no written language, no word for "book," and no alphabet. In a world with no paper and no writing utensils of any kind, they have no need for the literacy skills any second grader in America would take for granted.

Which means they have no Bible. No Bible, no church, no pastors, no knowledge of Jesus at all. They have never heard of Christ, let alone Christianity. My team and I aim to change that. This is year two of a twelve-year process, start to finish. We landed here knowing next to nothing. Between the six of us we knew about five Kilo words, but we were all fluent in Spanish, the trade language of Venezuela. We were told at least one of the Kilo people we met would be a Spanish speaker.

We were told wrong. No one here spoke Spanish. So, combined with the laughable amount of Kilo we knew, the task became almost impossible to consider. But we were too determined (or dumb maybe) to turn back. It took us two years of training at the Bible Institute, two years of language and cultural studies, and fifteen weeks of travel and government red tape to get here. We weren't going to be turned back by something as trivial as not being able to communicate.

One of the other missionaries, my friend Jeff, loves movies. Doesn't matter what's happening, he's got a movie quote for it. The day we learned that none of the Kilo spoke Spanish, we were all sitting around eating lunch, wondering what we had gotten ourselves into. Jeff took a big bite off his plate (sweet and sour rice, I think), swallowed and said, "We are too young to know that certain things are impossible. So we will do them anyway."

Apparently that's from some obscure Christian movie nobody but him has ever seen. But it didn't matter. What mattered was that afternoon we all pledged to not give up. Looking back on that moment now it seems pretty melodramatic, like something scripted for a Missions recruitment video. But we weren't trying to be dramatic and we weren't recruiting anyone but ourselves. We knew it would be hard, maybe impossible, and we decided to do it anyway. We'll see this thing through to the end—all for one and one for all.

Henry and his group don't stop to wait for me as they head down to the river, and I know I have to hurry. I duck my head inside the door and call out to Rachael.

"See you later, Babe!" I call in my best sing-song voice. "I'm going to work!"

"Okay, Honey! Be safe and be home before dinner!" comes her standard reply.

This is our little running joke, our little nod to the amusing absurdity of our "work" here. She knows I'm going fishing, but in my world fishing is work because the main part of my job right now is to learn the language and the culture. Making an accurate Bible translation means we have to be fluent in the Kilo language. The best way to be fluent? Spend time with the people. Today that means I'm going fishing.

So far I have become passably adept at speaking Kilo. No one would call me fluent, but I can hold my own in conversation and I can understand much of what is said around me. I have done a better job of acclimating to Kilo customs and culture, although I'm still pretty shaky on their history and folk lore.

Every time I lean in the door to tell my wife I'm going fishing (the most educational cultural activity there is here), I can't help but flash back to when I was a kid and would shout through the screen door to my mom that I was going down the street to a friend's house to play football.

I duck back outside and make my way around to the back of the house. Opening the door to the shed I pick out my best fishing spear from the selection along the wall. What? Don't tell me you only have one fishing spear!

I start to jog as I catch up to Henry and his crew. His name isn't Henry; of course, it's actually Mahala, which roughly translates to "Man of Hammer." When this was explained to me I was immediately reminded of the tall tales about John Henry we were taught in grammar-school history class. I'm not sure Mahala understood everything of what I told him about those American legends, but he was thrilled to be the first guy in the village with a "ghost name" and it has stuck with him ever since. "Ghost" is what many of the Kilo call me. Like a white spirit, they say. That's what the little kids thought we were when we walked up onto the riverbank that first day: white ghosts.

"Mister Neighbor, welcome," he says with a grin, as I catch up to the group and fall in step with them.

We are walking single file down the side of the airstrip in the traditional Kilo way. When you have to hack paths out of the jungle by hand, none of them ever become wide enough to walk side-by-side. I wonder what the Kilo would think of our sidewalks back home. Henry's smile is bigger than ever as he glances to take in the sweat that's beading on my forehead from running just thirty yards. Back home, sweating means you're working hard or you're out of shape. But for white men in the jungle, it usually just means you're outside after 11 am.

"Thanks, Henry. You don't mind if I come along, do you?"

I know the answer already, in Kilo culture it's rude to just insinuate yourself into a group without asking.

"Of course not, my friend. We always need an example of how to keep cool in the water!"

He laughs and so does the rest of the group. I grin right along with them, knowing that I deserve every bit of the abuse I'm about to take. Two weeks ago I was fishing with the guys when I slipped off the rock where I was perched. My dramatic splash into the water wasn't exactly a graceful swan dive. To make it worse, the fish I thought I was oh-so-close to spearing was actually well out of range, and they all saw it. The sweat from my brow had dripped into my eyes and obscured my vision. This messed with the already fragile depth perception that comes from looking down through the surface of the water. So I had tried to spear a fish that was comically far away.

While we walk, Henry and his friends amuse themselves for several minutes at my expense. Their reenactment of my fall is actually pretty good. I smile and take my medicine. More than simply enduring their banter, I revel in it. I revel in it because I understand their jabs and mocking to be exactly what they are: acceptance.

In Kilo culture the worst insult in the world is to ignore another person. To see a person wanting to join a group and not invite them in. Or to observe them in a dramatic moment and offer no comment. This would be tantamount to social exile. Strength is found in numbers and survival is based in the tribe. Isolation, then, is bad. That's one reason I can grin and bear their mockery. In the jungle of Venezuela, as in the locker rooms of America, guys show their affection by poking fun at each other. It means I am on the way to achieving my goal of becoming one of them.

We make our way down the side of the airstrip to what people back home would probably call "the beach." It isn't a beach in the traditional American sense of a place to go swimming, although swimming does happen there pretty much every day. It's much more than that; it's a secondary social hub. The primary social action takes place in the Commons, but the waterfront is a close second.

The path leading down from the airstrip is the widest here. Two people can pass each other going opposite directions, without having to step aside. Even with a full load of whatever they happen to be carrying, there's a bit of room to spare. For the women that usually means laundry, water, or children. For the men a typical load would be fish, firewood, or a canoe. From sunup to sundown the waterfront is typically a busy place, and today is no exception. Our little group, six in total, heads down the path on the left-hand side (something that took me almost an entire year to get used to), as a mother carrying her infant in a child loop with a water jug perched on top of her head makes her way past us.

In America we usually keep to the right, of course, but not here. The way it was explained to me is that you walk on the left-hand side of the trail as a defensive maneuver against potential attack. Even in the jungle most people are right-handed, and such a person walking on the right side of the trail would have a clumsy time bringing their weapon around quickly. So if you want to be ready for an adversary, you'd better walk on the left side of the trail. The logic makes sense, even though I have never seen even the slightest bit of violent aggression along any trail here.

This is because the Kilo are a prideful people, bound by honor codes as old as the jungle itself. To strike a person in the jungle is dishonorable because it gives the attacker the ability to hide and keep his actions a secret. Better to call out your opponent in the Commons so a public display can be made with witnesses on hand.

We emerge from the tree line and I take in the waterfront. From left to right the area is roughly fifty yards long, with a "beach" that covers probably ten yards from the tree line to the water. It's not really a beach in the way you're probably thinking. There's not much sand, just lots of rocks and a few grassy areas here and there. It's mostly an area where the jungle is not, rather than an area where something else is. But "beach" is the best word I have for it, so that's what we call it.

The Kilo call it Piebu.

The Place.

The best I can discern, it is called The Place mostly because this is where the action happens during the day. I see women washing clothes by dunking them in the water and slapping them on rocks. There are many misconceptions about life in the jungle, but this is not one of them. These women are the very picture of jungle people that Americans have in their minds.

Small children play in the water near their mothers, careful not to stray too far away from the bank. There's not much of a current, but it wouldn't take much to overpower a three-year-old. Older kids are scattered down the shoreline in groups of one or two. I watch as they tread carefully, bent at the waist. Occasionally one will reach down and yank up a rock, while the other one, quick as lightening, shoots a hand down into the water to pluck up a small creature. I can never remember the word for what they're catching, but it looks like a mini-crawfish to me.

I glance across the water and down the river about a hundred yards, and see our destination. Just before a sharp curve in the river, the water eddies almost to a standstill in a rocky cove where fish get trapped. They get pushed in with the current and for some reason many can't get back out. So they stay there until we come to get them out. Back home in the States I'm sure some environmentalists would have a conniption if they knew that the Kilo have fished in this exact same spot for the exact same type of fish for generations. No catch and release, no permits, and no daily quotas. Yet, as we wade into the water and begin to float downstream, I know there will be fish there.

As I kick my legs gently and swim through the water, I rehearse how to correctly pronounce the word for what I call the cove: bahweetan. It means "fish home," because it's where the fish live. An effective name, if not very creative.

Our little group swims into the cove and I wonder exactly what event in nature could have happened that caused these large rocks to be plunked down in this particular spot. No doubt an evolutionist would see the work of some ancient glacier in the remote past, while a pulpit-thumping preacher would credit God's hand. I land somewhere in the middle. I have serious doubts about the theory of evolution, but I also don't think God is in the business of moving rocks around one by one. And they're way too big for the Kilo to have done it.

When I asked Henry how the cove got to be the way it is, he just shrugged and said, "Nimishish."

That's a fairly common Kilo word roughly equivalent to the English phrase "I couldn't care less." It expresses the idea that there are some things in life that are so trivial or abstract, they don't really matter. Geology holds little interest for people who don't have enough to eat.

"Why would a man ponder rocks," Henry asked, "when there are fish to be speared?"

Touché.

We spread out and take up familiar positions as Henry sprinkles bugs around the water. He dips into a pouch at his waist, dropping about a dozen insects onto the surface. It takes a minute or two, but soon enough the fish start to appear. One by one, heads poke out from cracks and crags and then dart up to the surface. We let the first two get away, with no one even attempting a strike. After that, all bets are off.

Henry is by far the best at spearing fish, and he quickly manages to score six kills. Soon enough everyone is finished and we assemble on the bank. We sling mesh bags around our shoulders, with the newly cleaned fish inside. The river will wash away any remaining blood or scales as we swim home. The current is not strong, but even so I labor to make it upstream.

The last to arrive back, I wade onto shore and fall in as the women and children head up the trail. The men have not waited for me, and I don't blame them. I see their backs disappearing up the trail and I know they mean no offense. It's common sense actually. Why stand around on the shore when your dinner is on your back? If I ever outswim any of them I'll do the same, but I don't think they're worried about that ever happening.

Rachael has a fire going outside and she looks up as I cross the yard toward her. We cook the fish camp-style over the coals, wrapping them in foil with onions and butter. Twenty minutes later we are eating quietly as dusk settles onto the village and the shadows grow long.

That night I fall asleep in an introspective mood. I may be living in the jungle, and the football game I watched today was on a DVD mailed from home, but I wonder: *How many men have what I have? I live in a beautiful place with a beautiful woman. I have more food than I can eat, free time to pursue hobbies I enjoy, and a job that is rewarding and beneficial. How many men are stuck on a corporate hamster wheel, fishing for what I have already managed to catch? Who knows, and frankly, right now I couldn't care less. Nimishish, as Henry would say.*

Nimishish.

## Chapter 3

Monday morning dawns bright and early, and that's no cliché. Since it gets bright so early here, and they have no electricity, life for the Kilo falls into rhythm with nature—they rise and retire with the sun.

I learned a long time ago that aside from fishing trips, the best time for language learning is in the Commons just after breakfast. So most days I'm up with the sun (now do you understand why sleeping in was so important yesterday?). My morning routine looks pretty much like many other working man's routine: an alarm clock, a snooze button, coffee, a shower, more coffee, breakfast, more coffee, and out the door for work. I honestly have no idea how people live without coffee. I'm not picky about what kind—coffee snobs wouldn't last in the jungle—it just has to be hot and caffeinated. Back home in the States people sometimes ask how I can drink coffee in the jungle.

"Isn't it too hot for coffee?" they ask.

If you ever run across such a person, be polite, but get away from them as fast as you can. Like the decaf crazies I mentioned earlier, they clearly don't under-stand coffee and cannot be trusted.

The Commons is like a town square. It is located on the edge of the village and serves as the place to conduct public business. Marriages are conducted here, healing services, baby purification rites, and sometimes even arguments are settled by traditional (meaning violent) means, if no other solution has been found.

As I round the corner to the Commons, I take in the scene: roughly twenty-five yards square (I say "roughly" because there is no such thing as a perfect square, or even a straight line, in the jungle) and bordered on three sides by rustic buildings, the church being one of them. It looks exactly like it does every day. I pass a small group of women discussing their gardens as they prepare to head out for the morning's work. Their conversation floats to my ears and I translate as I walk, trying not to be too obvious.

"Today I must finish the third row. If not, my husband will be angry."

"Angry? How will he know? When was the last time you saw a husband in the gardens?"

"True, I know, but I cannot lie to him. Even if my words lie, my face will tell the truth and he will..."

Their words fade as I move out of earshot. I pass two boys fighting with sticks. This kind of play is common to boys everywhere who want to grow up to be men and warriors. I wave a greeting to the Blue Haired Biddies, a cluster of old women so frail they no longer do garden work or haul water like the rest of the women. Now they spend the days clucking their tongues at anything they disapprove of, and fussing over little children. It is a cultural honor to be one of them, but I sense the women themselves wish for more productive times. Supposedly no one has ever lived longer than two years after joining their ranks, and my guess is that after a lifetime of work, the stillness more or less kills them. (It should go without saying that I am the only person who calls them the Blue Haired

Biddies, and that only in my head.)

"Mister Neighbor!"

I hear this above the din, recognizing Henry's voice and being reminded of how he was the first Kilo to befriend the new guy in town when we arrived. Most of the people were understandably wary of us. Not until an entire year went by did we learn that they called us *simbee* behind our backs.

Ghosts.

Henry was different. He welcomed us quickly and has been a godsend. He soon became an invaluable help not only as a friend, but also as a language consultant. When we finally manage to finish the Kilo Bible we've started, it will have Henry's fingerprints all over it. He has spent countless hours in my office with me, patiently pronouncing words and making sure I get the inflections just right. The ability of Kilo people to understand the Bible will hinge on our ability to understand their language, so it has to be perfect.

"Good morning, Henry," I reply, taking his wrist once again. "What's the plan for today?"

"We are clearing land for new gardens in the morning, but when the sun gets angry I plan to go back for more Cantu. I will not cook myself in the sun today—you may come too."

"I wish I could, Henry. But I must work inside today."

I can tell by his grin that Henry is about to give me a hard time, probably something along the lines of "only women work inside," but a sudden commotion in another part of the Commons interrupts our conversation.

"Mister Neighbor," someone yells at me from over there, "Come learn this!"

I have left standing instructions with the villagers to come get me whenever something unusual happens. Spear fishing is common, and thus an easily learned part of Kilo life. Other things are not so common. In fact, some of the most important parts of Kilo life may occur only once in a great while. Based on the tone of the words, I'm hopeful this is one of those times. I hustle over to the people gathered around the man who shouted. It's Bigfoot, the neighbor who doesn't understand football.

"What is it?" I ask as I lean in.

"Dadu," Bigfoot replies.

I can smell the dadu before I even see it. *Dadu* is the Kilo word for…how can I say this politely? Poop. Okay, that wasn't very polite, but you get the point.

"I can see that," I reply. "Why do I need to learn this? I have already learned dadu."

"Not this. This is Wapa dadu."

*Wapa* is a word I know nothing about. In two years of living in the jungle I've never heard it before. My face betrays my confusion and Bigfoot begins to explain.

"The Wapa only comes when it wants to come. But when it comes we must find it."

"So the Wapa is an animal?" I ask, wondering exactly what makes this thing so special that they *must* find it.

"Yes, but not just any animal. The helper animal that no longer helps. Our ancestors tell us it was the Wapa who gave them this place. The Wapa gave

Bahwee to the Kilo. Our ancestors believed that the land must be given by the ones who arrived first. The Wapa were here before the Kilo. It was the Wapa who gave us land and left it for us."

"Okay, but how come I've never…"

My words get cut off by Henry. He is excited, bordering on ecstatic. He did not follow me across the Commons at first, but now he approaches the group, his whole face having lit up when he heard about the Wapa.

"Tell the women! Call the children! Today is a great day!"

"No," Bigfoot replies, taking Henry by the shoulders. "Today is the *best* day."

They run off, lost in an excitement that I'm completely unable to share. I look around the Commons and see activity everywhere. To my eyes it seems as if every person in the village is simultaneously entering and leaving the Commons. People flow through the area at a frantic pace. Teenagers carry supplies. Men strap on machetes and bows with quivers full of arrows. There is more food than I have ever seen at one time and I wonder where it came from. The women are busy with what I can only guess is packing lunches. Each set of a mother and her daughters is laying aside bundles of bread and fruit. The children, well, I'm not sure what to say about them.

Some of the boys are play-fighting, shooting mock arrows at one particular kid who is crawling on all fours. He pantomimes being hit with an arrow and the others actually make a show pretending to chase him out of the area. One little boy was not so careful.

In the chase he runs smack into the legs of his mother and is immediately rewarded with a scolding. Based on the look of his face and the way he walks dejectedly toward the village, I can fill in the blanks on my own.

For my part, I have no idea what to do. People continue to pour in and out of the Commons in an almost liquid way. The whole tribe seems to be acting in concert toward a single goal. I'm frozen in place. The villagers swarm around me like a rock in a stream. Unlike a rock, however, I am not unmovable, and a couple boys on the pretend hunt jostle the back of my legs enough to make me lose my balance. I stumble a couple quick steps back and almost hit the dirt. I regain my balance just as everyone seems to disappear. The quiet that now descends on the square is so sudden, it's eerie.

I love Western movies. Clint Eastwood. John Wayne. Roy Rogers. Even Russell Crowe made a couple decent ones. Pretty much any movie where the cowboy saves the day by shooting the outlaw is good by me. Sorry for the abrupt change of subject there, it's just that in the moment of sudden quiet, I am reminded of those old movies. You know how it always goes: High Noon on Main Street. The gunslinger faces off against the cattle rustler. Everyone else in town disappears into the background, leaving the two men staring daggers at each other. Fingers twitch over holsters. Sweat drips down their necks as tumbleweeds swirl around their ankles. A pregnant pause with a melodramatic soundtrack playing in the background...

That pregnant pause is what this moment feels like as I stand there in the deserted Commons. I can feel a breeze gently cooling the sweat I didn't even realize had broken out across my forehead. I picture Clint Eastwood from *The Good, The Bad, and The Ugly.* The Man with No Name. That's me right now. I squint. I cock my head to the side against the sun. I look expectantly across the square, anticipating the appearance of my outlaw enemy. All of these connect-the-dots thoughts flash through my head in the half second it takes me to straighten up from my stumble. My eyes focus into the middle distance. I look and I see...

The Blue Haired Biddies.

Kind of a letdown, I'll admit. Then again my imagination regularly outpaces reality.

Everyone else has apparently found somewhere else to be, because the Biddies and a few stray kids are the only people around at the moment. Not knowing what else to do, I amble nonchalantly over to where the Biddies sit in a group, each of them perched on a tree stump. It's their regular meeting place and they can be found here each morning.

"Puin-a," I say softly, trying to seem normal. As if the whole village didn't just lose its collective mind over dadu. Granted, it's a fairly large pile of dadu, but it's still not something to get excited about. *Puin-a* is a fairly standard Kilo greeting. It says hello and how's it going, all at the same time. A jungle version of "What's up?"

"Puin-a ye," one of the old ladies responds, returning my greeting. Basically she answered my question of "What's up?" with "What's up with you?"

One of the quirks about Kilo language is what I call The Boomerang Effect. Quite often in conversation the phrases returned in reply to a question are a rephrasing of the original question you just asked. It reminds me of those irritating teachers I had as a kid. If they asked on a test, "Who was the first President of the United States?" You couldn't answer "George Washington." That would be too simple. If you wanted full credit you had to answer, "The first President of the United States was George Washington."

To this day I have no idea why they made us do that. Maybe it was an anti-cheating scheme or something. You know, camouflage your answer in a forest of other words to make it harder to read over somebody else's shoulder. Whatever. I don't know, and frankly, I don't care. I bring it up because Kilo conversation can be like that. Especially in formal settings when a younger person (that's me) is talking with an older person (the Biddies). The question gets restated and returned to the original asker—hence The Boomerang Effect. Weird, but effective as a social device. To not engage this way would convey disrespect. Unless the two people talking are equals. Then it's perfectly fine to just write "George Washington," without restating the question.

Confused yet?

Yeah, me too. But I'm working on it. I'll probably never get to where I automatically know this stuff without thinking, but I'm coming along nicely. This whole thing is totally off the topic of my conversation with the Biddies though—stop distracting me.

I'm still trying to figure out where everyone went and what, exactly, is a Wapa. Take that little snippet of what I just tried to explain to you and multiply it to the tenth power and you'll get a picture of what it's like trying to learn a language and a culture in the jungle. Confusing at first, but once you get the hang of it things go a little easier.

I won't bore you with the translation of every word and phrase I exchange with the Biddies. The English gist of it goes something like this.

"What's up?"

"What's up with you?" I asked the question, but because I have less social standing than the old ladies, the question gets boomeranged back for me to answer first.

"I have many questions."

"We have many answers. What troubles you?"

"Where have all the people gone?"

In the two seconds it takes the Biddies to silently look at each other and determine who is going to answer my question (another social ritual I don't understand yet), a song pops into my head. I've been living in the jungle for two years. I haven't been back to visit the United States in almost a year. Yet, as soon as the phrase "Where have all the people gone" passes through my lips, a song pops into my head. Best guess? I heard it on the bus in junior high.

It's Paula Cole mournfully wondering, *Where have all the Cowboys goooone?*

I wish I was making this up. I'm not. My ADD is really just that bad.

"They have gone from here," comes the reply from the oldest of the Biddies, saving me from finishing the rest of the song in my mind.

Instead I think, *Thanks, Captain Obvious. As if I*

*couldn't see that on my own.*

"…to prepare for the journey to chase the sun," she finishes.

"Chase the sun? Who is chasing the sun?"

"The Wapa."

"The Wapa live chasing the sun?"

"The Wapa live chasing the sun because the Kilo live toward the sun."

In case you're not following the logic here, "toward the sun" is how the Kilo say "east" and "chasing the sun" is how they say "west." It seems odd at first, but once you get used to it, it makes a certain amount of sense.

"What are the Wapa?"

"The Wapa are the giving creature. They gifted this jungle to the Kilo. We owe what we have to the Wapa. They gave all so that we may have some."

Okay, at this point I'm going to skip the back-and-forth for you. The Biddies and I have a long conversation about the Wapa. Supato, the oldest lady who does most of the talking, has apparently been designated as their leader because none of the other ladies say much at all. She struggles to talk, rarely getting out more than a sentence or two at a time before losing her breath. The result is a very stilted and halting conversation.

But here's what I learned.

The Kilo legend passed down from long ago says that the Wapa lived in all parts of the jungle. They roamed freely over the earth, intermingling with the Kilo. No one killed each other. No one had to worry. Peace and harmony all around. Just everyone living together in beautiful bliss. It was starting to sound like a John Lennon song, until Supato got to the main point. The Kilo grew in numbers until it became apparent that they needed to separate. The Wapa are not what you would call prolific breeders. They live very long lives and have babies only infrequently. Bottom line, the Kilo were pushing the Wapa out of their own land. Their existence was threatened. What to do?

At this point I should probably mention that Supato is speaking of the Wapa as if they were human. I learned a long time ago in English class this has something to do with "anthroprofessions" or something like that. Whatever the word for it, it's pretty common in Kilo culture to talk about things in nature as if they were companions or peers.

Anyway, apparently some of the Wapa wanted to eliminate the problem by killing the Kilo. Lucky for the Kilo, the idea went nowhere. Most of the Wapa loved the Kilo and did not want to kill them. Instead they agreed to gift this jungle to the people, choosing instead to remove themselves in the direction of the setting sun. To the west.

Unfortunately, this legend doesn't have the happiest of endings. The small group of Wapa that originally wanted to eliminate the Kilo did not actually change their minds, they just got outvoted. The Wapa moved west, including the violent-minded ones. To this day the elusive Wapa remain in the west, with the exception of occasional forays back east by the disaffected Wapa intent on wiping out the Kilo and recapturing their homeland jungle.

The appearance of Wapa signs (such as dadu) indicate to the Kilo that a rogue Wapa has journeyed back east in an attempt to move against the Kilo. The Kilo system of keeping time is pretty hazy and non-specific, but the best I was able to gather, today marks the first Wapa sighting in at least a generation. This explains why everybody freaked out and rushed off, leaving me scratching my head.

The Biddies are tired. Supato looks spent. I feel bad for having exhausted her with my questions, but only a little. Before I leave them to rest, Supato gathers one more burst of breath and her frail hand reaches out and grasps my elbow.

"Be careful, Ghost. Wapa do not come alone."

Four questions later, I learn that the legend of the Wapa also tells us they always enlist the help of snakes. Sounds eerie, but also not likely. I've been here for two years and at this point I have seen exactly zero snakes. Everybody back home assumes the jungle is crawling with them, but nothing could be further from the truth.

In fact, I encountered more snakes back home in Michigan than I have in the jungle here. So the idea that the Wapa would somehow enlist the help of snakes makes no sense to me. I guess that's why nobody ever asks white guys to write jungle myths.

At any rate, Supato is worn out, slumping badly to the point that I hope the effort won't actually kill her. Talk about a lousy prayer letter. "This month I had the privilege of learning local folklore from a respected village elder. She died as a result of our conversation."

That's not exactly the type of report that helps boost support from back home. I *really* hope she's just tired!

## Chapter 4

"Hey, Babe!" Rachael greets me with a kiss as I walk through the door. "What was all the excitement about? I heard everybody shouting but then they all rushed home. Before I could find out what was happening, the men disappeared into the jungle. They took the west trail on the other side of the airstrip."

"Wapa dadu," I reply matter-of-factly, as if that explains everything.

"Um....?" She knows what dadu is, but like me, had never heard of the Wapa.

I talk her through everything that happened that morning, including my conversation with the old lady, Supato.

"That's crazy," she says. "I've never heard that."

"Yeah, me neither. But it makes sense."

"Even Matrudi never brought it up, and she talks about *everything*."

Matrudi is the town gossip. She and Rachael often sit together in the afternoons to chat. Rachael doesn't like to gossip, and tries to change the subject when things get too personal. The thing is, though, talking with Matrudi has really sped up Rachael's language acquisition.

"She might not ever think about it," I explain. "Supato said the angry Wapa are so few in number that they only venture east once every generation or so. She might not know anything about it."

"She is still pretty young—at least I think so. Probably not more than thirty."

The Kilo keep track of time based on the harvesting of fruit. Cordaleet is a jungle fruit that is ready for harvest roughly twice a year. Similar to a passion fruit in size and taste, it grows with such consistent regularity around here that it's the one source of food the Kilo do not have to work hard at getting. If you ask how old a person is, their parents will reply by telling you how many cordaleet seasons have come and gone since their birth.

"He was born two handfuls of cordaleet ago."

"Two handfuls" equals 10, and because we know that cordaleet is ready to harvest roughly every six months, that means the kid in question is about five years old. I should emphasize "about," because shortly after I arrived in the jungle I started to keep close track, and it turns out the cordaleet harvest cycle is just shy of six months. Three weeks shy usually. For people with no calendar, no clocks, and no need for precise dates of any kind, that's not a problem. But for a slightly OCD American like me, it's enough to be distracting.

"So I guess this means an indoor work day, huh?" Rachael says.

"Yeah, I was planning to spend the whole day on translation work, but I've already lost half of it. Maybe I'll just work on vocab instead. What are you gonna do today?" I ask this as I pull up the translation software on my laptop.

"I'm almost done with the belly wrap for Nipatu," she says, indicating the pile of cloth on the end table. "I think I can finish before dinner."

Since moving to the jungle Rachael has become quite a seamstress. What started as a way to spend time chatting with neighbors has turned into a cottage industry for her. The belly wrap is a cloth/elastic hybrid she invented. I honestly have no idea how she makes them or why it works. I only know it does.

Being pregnant does not mean a Kilo woman gets to stay home and just chill by the fire. She still hauls water, cooks food, cares for children, and tends the garden. You can imagine how it feels to work like that when you're pregnant. High blood pressure and back problems are the norm among women in the village. Rachael is trying to change all that with her belly wrap.

Like I said, I have no idea how she makes them or how it works. I can break down and rebuild a motorcycle engine. I can update translation software, build a shed, clear trees for a runway, and a hundred other useful things. But I don't know the first thing about clothes or sewing. Yeah, I'm a regular enlightened modern guy, I know.

Somehow the cloth and elastic work together in a push-pull tandem of pressure and weight distribution. The effect is that the constant pressure on their lower back is eased and the incessant pull on their growing belly is likewise helped. All of the women were super hesitant at first, but they are starting to come around to the idea, and the idea is catching on.

This is great for Rachael. It is also bad for Rachael. Great, because it builds relationships and meets a real need in a new way. Bad, because each one has to be custom fit and custom measured. There is no one-size-fits-all option. In a culture with no birth control and strong societal pressure to have a large family, there is a new pregnancy in the village just about every month, so Rachael has been quite busy.

"That's great," I say, as I slip on my headphones and go to work.

Rachael wrings out the dish cloth she was using to clean up the kitchen, and heads for the chair in the corner of the living room. Just before the noise-canceling headphones envelope me in silence, I am struck by the fact I may not even need them this time. Normally the village outside is full of activity and noise. But not today.

All the men left in search of the Wapa and the women have a holiday of sorts. I've never seen the village so devoid of activity. Still, out of habit I leave the headphones on. They help me concentrate on the new list of words Henry helped me translate the week before. My task today is the painstaking process of categorizing and listing them all. The language database we are compiling is, literally, one-of-a-kind. Everything has to be perfect. It might sound overly dramatic to put it this way, but it's not really—the souls of the Kilo people depend on it. If our translation is off in significant ways, they may not get the chance to understand God's Word for themselves.

***

The afternoon wears on and I'm in a rare zone. Normally my attention span is short and I take frequent breaks during translation work, but today I am abnormally focused. Eventually I glance over my shoulder to where Rachael was working and see a pretty bag tied off with a colorful bow. Nobody around here has ever heard of a baby shower, but that doesn't stop her from celebrating every new birth. She's the best.

I stand up and stretch, looking around the house. Her dinner plan is obvious: pork chops on the counter next to a bowl of fresh beans. Onions and garlic are to the side on a separate plate and my stomach starts to make noise. Actual grumbles. Apparently it didn't realize it was empty until my eyes saw the food.

Rachael comes back inside through the front door.

"Welcome back to the land of the living. You were really getting after it today."

"I know, right? I can't remember the last time I worked that long without a sanity break."

She picks up the wrapped bundle from the table.

"I'm headed over to Nipatu's. If you can start the grill I should be back about the time dinner's ready."

She leaves and I walk out back to start the charcoal for the grill. It's another of those good/bad things about living here. With no propane filling stations anywhere, we grill with charcoal. Which is great, because the meat tastes better that way. Also not great, because it takes forever to heat up. Back in the States I never had to wait for the grill to heat up. Turn on the burners, throw in a match, and inside of three minutes everything is hot and ready to go. With charcoal it's a thirty-minute process.

Yes, I really am grumbling about a half-hour wait for dinner. Even here in the Third World I've still got First World problems. Brought them along with me, I guess.

As I go about lighting the charcoal, I think about the missionary partners who came over from the First World with us. Jeff and Wendy were part of our original team here in Venezuela. We met at the Bible training institute where we did our pre-field studies. At the time none of us knew where we would end up on the mission field, just that we wanted jungle work. The four of us hit it off right away and it didn't take long to come up with the idea that we should go to the same field. Several years later and here we all are. Jeff is easily my best friend in the world and it still amazes me that two people who are so different can get along so well.

And a good thing too. The number one reason why missionaries leave the field is because they can't get along with each other. Seriously. I'm not even kidding. They can live in the jungle, eat weird food in foreign cities, and learn new languages, but all too often they just can't get along. I heard one time that some 70 percent of missionaries who don't make it to the end of their first term cite "team member conflicts" as their reason for going home. Crazy, huh?

When the charcoal is lit I head into the house to get the meat ready. There's nothing more American than grilling meat for dinner. As I prepare the chops I am once again struck by how many things about life in the jungle are so very normal. To be sure, much of my life is light years away from the life I knew back home. Not all of it though. I watch football on Sundays. I grill meat for dinner. I have friends over to play cards. I check my email every morning and again every night. I.... You get the picture. Growing up we heard such horrible stories about life on the mission field, it's a wonder anyone went at all. I'm not saying life in the jungle is a breeze; it's just not as bad as I thought it would be. So far.

One thing most Americans wouldn't like is how we can't surf the web and how frustratingly slow our radio-based email service is. As you can imagine, there are no cell towers in the jungle and the nearest Internet Service Provider is several hundred miles away. Our home office has been in negotiation with a new satellite internet startup who will supposedly be providing us with internet service in the near future, but I'm not holding my breath. If it happens, great—a little faster communication would be nice. Right now it can take a day, sometimes two, for a response. But honestly, I don't mind. There's something liberating about not being immediately available to anyone and everyone who wants your attention.

When the chops are pounded, I season them liberally and then start to work on the onions and garlic. I mash the garlic with the side of my knife and rub it into the meat, mixing it with the seasoning and getting it all over my hands. The onions get chopped into big pieces and tossed with oil and garlic. Everything is going on the grill because we try not to cook inside. Another thing we don't have out here in the jungle is air conditioning, so we use the grill outside as much as we can.

The chops sizzle as I lay them on the grate. Nothing sounds better than meat sizzling on a hot grill! Just before our first flight to the mission field I heard about a celebrity chef back home who likes to go to crazy, out-of-the-way places and eat native food with the people who live there. Apparently there's nowhere he won't go. I'd love to have him come to this jungle! Man, could I show him some good food he's never going to find anywhere else. Literally nowhere else. I'm making a traditional American dinner right now, but some of the stuff the Kilo have fed me is exotic with a capital E, like fire-roasted shrub grubs, anteater jerky, and a dish I can never pronounce correctly that reminds me of a potato pancake. That last one sounds pretty blasé until you learn that if the person preparing it makes a mistake in any of the seven essential steps, it comes out poisonous. That's no joke. It is one intense pancake.

When I flip the chops, I add the onions and the beans to the grill. Rachael comes around the side of the house just then. She ducks inside, grabs some plates, and makes up the picnic table for two. When everything on the grill is done, I pile it onto a platter and join my wife at the picnic table.

"What did Nipatu think of the belly wrap?" I ask, as I slide into the seat opposite to her.

"She was really unsure at first," she says. "But all of them usually are. By the time I left she was starting to come around."

"I can't say I blame her. I sure wouldn't trust some lady who wanted to make underwear for me!"

"That's the thing," she says, "they didn't, remember? At first none of them would even look at it. Just convincing them to give it a chance was impossible."

"Oh, I remember," I say as I laugh at the memory of one particular tribal lady who tried to burn the belly wrap when Rachael wasn't looking. A month of sewing literally gone up in smoke.

"But now," she goes on, "there were three other women there today, helping me fit Nipatu into hers."

She does the air quote thing around the word *helping* as she talks.

"The thing is though, I didn't mind," Rachael continues, turning serious. "They weren't any help with the fitting, of course, but I don't think Nipatu would have tried it on if they weren't there to tell her how helpful it would be. It really means a lot."

In our training we were so filled with gung-ho enthusiasm, we didn't really pay much attention to the veteran missionaries who tried to tell us how important it would be to build relationships with the Kilo. Oh, we said we understood, of course. In reality though, we were just paying lip service to the concept of relationship-building. We had no idea. How could we? We had never lived in a tribe before. We had never started friendships from scratch, building from the ground up. Even as kids growing up there was always the common ground of a neighborhood to work with. Or a sports team. Simply growing up in the same place can form bonds between people. In the jungle there is none of that.

To hear that there were three women from the tribe who not only showed up to "help" Rachael, but also backed her up in the conversation? That means a lot. That's truly what it's about—the relationships. The idea is slowly catching on, and I do mean slowly. Not all the pregnant ladies from the tribe have taken her up on the idea. They aren't being mean; it's just that undergarments are pretty much unheard of here, let alone some elastic girdle-like thing.

"These chops are delicious." Rachael says, interrupting my scattered thoughts. "I'm so glad I married a man who can cook." She gives me a little wink and I can't help but smile, even though she is totally making fun of me. Seriously, she is just irresistible!

Truth be told, I can't cook anything that doesn't come off the grill.

We chow our way through dinner, not really talking all that much. Not because we don't have much to say, but because we don't normally talk and eat at the same time. I don't like to toot my own horn, but the chops really are delicious. The pork is what a foodie back home would call "GMO-free organic." Which just means the hogs are raised the old-fashioned way—without growth hormones. The Kilo are not much for animal husbandry, but Jeff and I have started raising a few pigs on our own. They're great because they'll eat anything and we can pretty much ignore them until we're ready to slaughter one or two. At first the Kilo looked at us like we were from Mars.

"You will live with animals?" one guy asked.

"Not live with them," Jeff tried to explain. "They will live outside and we will take care of them, but they won't come in the house."

"That is good. I would not trust a man who lived with animals. It would be unnatural."

At that point Jeff looked a question over at me. In the silent three seconds that we shared a glance, it was like a whole conversation happened by telepathy and raised eyebrows.

*"We should tell him about American pets."*

*"Are you nuts? They barely trust us now."*

*"Yeah, but can you imagine the look on his face when he hears about people who live with cats and dogs?"*

*"Leave your crazy aunt and her seven sweater-wearing cats out of this. Nobody needs to know about that."*

*"You're probably right. But you gotta admit, it would be fun."*

*"We can tell him some other time."*

*"Yeah okay, you're right."*

Since then Jeff and I have successfully raised and slaughtered two hogs. We originally started with six, but three of them didn't make it. One died shortly after we got them in the pen. One managed to squirm away from a neighbor kid who wanted to hold it, running off into the jungle. We never saw him again. The piglet I mean, not the neighbor kid. The third one just disappeared. We woke one day and it was gone. The shaman claims it was taken by spirits, but more than likely it just found a way out of the pen somehow. An optimist would hope it would come home. A realist knows that's an impossible thing to hope for. There isn't much hope for a domesticated pig in the jungle. That leaves us with one still in the pen, and we're hoping for a few more with the next supply plane.

The supply plane comes once a month and there is no telling what will be on it. What arrives will be things we requested from the mission base in the city, so there will be no surprises there. The unknown part will be exactly which of the things we requested were available, along with how long ago we requested them. Supply buying is a whole other world of missionary logistics that I don't even know the half of. Our mission employs two full-time people whose entire job is to keep records of which missionaries need what supplies. They live in cities and serve any missionary within flying distance. Their job is to make sure missionaries in jungle stations have what we need to stay and work. They coordinate with the Finance Department to pay for the supplies they purchase, drawing funds out of our accounts as necessary, as well as the Aviation Department. The fliers deliver the stuff to us in the jungle, along with the mail bag. That makes those guys pretty popular.

Before I became a missionary, I had no idea how complicated the whole thing is. I had this romanticized picture in my head of boarding a ship for some far-off land. I would sail with my wife and our suitcases into unknown territory, just us and Jesus against the heathen unbelief of the world. In reality, for every missionary in the jungle who's translating and preaching, there are at least twenty-five other missionaries working behind the scenes to make it possible. You don't have to translate or preach to be a missionary. Maybe you're good with computers, or numbers, or medicine. We need those types of people too.

"Look at that sunset," Rachael says as she stacks up our plates to carry them inside. "I've got to get a picture. My dad would love it."

Rachael and her dad love to talk about the weather. I don't get it, but it's their thing. The first thing her dad will ask about when we call from the city is, "How's the weather?" Then he'll tell her about what it's like back in Michigan. Tornadic activity. Freezing fog. Straight Line Winds. I'm not kidding. These are actual words they use.

I tease her about it, but the fact is, I'm just not smart enough to get it. I spent more time sleeping in science class than taking notes. So their weather conversations just go right over my head. But even a Neanderthal like me can appreciate the sky above us right now. The clouds are especially high up in the atmosphere tonight and the colors are remarkable. Reds and yellows mix into something that I can only call an unnatural purple. Yes, even I know that red and yellow don't make purple. That's why I say it's unnatural. Even still, it's right there in front of me for the entire world to see. I'm sure there is some technical phrase for it, but I'll just call it cool.

Rachael comes back outside with the camera and snaps a few pictures. She scrolls through to pick the best one, deleting the rest.

"Come here," she says, beckoning me over to where there is a clear sight line to the sunset. "Let's get a picture—this will be perfect for the cover photo on our next Prayer Profile."

Lots of people say they hate selfies, but then they take them all the time anyway. I actually do hate selfies. There is only one person in the whole world I will take them for, and that's Rachael. I love her more than I hate selfies, so I smile as we push our heads together and she snaps off a few pictures. The shot is perfect, framed by a tall tree on one side and the sunset on the other.

We finish the rest of the evening with unremarkable activities. We wash the dishes. We check our email, drumming our fingers because the radio-based system is so slow. Rachael saves the selfie in a folder for our next Prayer Profile. While she works on the computer

I read a book in the chair. Put a pipe in my hand and a dog at my feet and I'd look like a Norman Rockwell painting come to life.

The Prayer Profile is our attempt at Missions innovation. Since the dawn of modern missions, I think all prayer letters home from the field have looked the same: a posed picture of a perfect and smiling missionary family. Neckties cinched up tight (as if anyone wears a necktie in the jungle) in an outdated picture pasted above a by-the-numbers update on the incredibly exciting and important work they've been doing. A list of prayer requests to make George Mueller jealous. And always a hint at needing more support.

Not ours. We were inspired by missionaries from our church that sent us a prayer card when we were in high school. They were camp missionaries and their prayer card featured a giant T-Rex chasing them across the grounds. Easily the best prayer card I've ever seen. I wanted to be like that guy. I wanted to be different. I wanted to be remembered by our people back home. Not so I could be famous or anything like that, but so they would actually pray for me. You can't pray for someone you forget about, and I wanted our prayer cards to be unforgettable.

So we modeled our Prayer Profile on a popular social networking site. There are pictures, but not boring posed shots from some cookie-cutter studio back home. We put in a new picture of ourselves in the field every time, along with an "action" shot of some Kilo from the village. No neckties allowed, ever. There are prayer requests, but not the sanitized and smoothed-over kind. For example, one month we asked for prayer because a neighboring Kilo was really annoying us and it was getting harder and harder to simply be nice. He kept insisting my motorcycle was evil and during the night he would move it out of my yard and into the jungle. Only by the prayers of our people back home did I manage to be consistently polite with him.

Rachael finishes up the new Prayer Profile just about the time I finish being awake. I'm dozing off in the chair, and she's ready for bed too, and so we turn off the lights and head down the hall. As I lay in bed staring into the dark, I reflect on the nature of my job again. Aside from the rush of the morning there was nothing exciting that happened yesterday or today. I worked on the computer. My wife did some sewing. She emailed her dad and I read a book. On the one hand, this is somewhat disappointing for a guy who fancies himself a Jungle Missionary. On the other hand, I am totally okay with it. I have always been a routine sort of person. I saw a guy once with a t-shirt that said, *"If you're not living on the edge you're taking up too much space!"*

I have never thought like that. I don't mind a little excitement and adventure now and again (who doesn't?), but I've never been the type to crave a lot of danger. In fact, I'd rather avoid it if possible.

Thinking about things this way, I wonder if I've been too hard on the office types back home at Headquarters. If I'm honest with myself I have to admit—life as a jungle missionary is more routine than not. I'm okay with that, so maybe I should do what they want and adopt the name "Tribal Missionary" instead.

Maybe.

## Chapter 5

Another routine day goes by, and the men are still out in the jungle. I've honestly never heard of this happening. Not here with the Kilo, and not in any other tribe our mission works with. Hunting trips and gathering parties rarely go away for more than a day or two at most. Whenever the cordaleet is ripe the Kilo will camp out in the jungle where it grows and live there for a while during the harvest, but that's different. When they do that they call it Buntai. It's a Kilo word that has no real English counterpart. It means to leave your home for a lengthy period of time expecting to return. Whenever the Kilo go to the jungle and harvest cordaleet, they say they are Buntai. As a noun we say they are "on Buntai."

Okay, okay, you get it—enough with the grammar lesson already. Suffice it to say that the men being gone so long right now is not a case of Buntai come early.

Other than Buntai, forty-eight hours is the max I have ever known a Kilo group to be away, and we have almost hit that point. At first their absence was kind of nice. I'm probably not supposed to tell you this, but living in the village can be exhausting. Don't get me wrong, I love it. It's just that any job, no matter how much you love it, becomes tiring after a while and you need a break. For me, these last couple days have been that break.

Now though, it's starting to get weird.

Rachael and I are sitting around the table with Jeff and Wendy, having dinner Wednesday night. Over dinner we talk about hopefully getting a new shipment of piglets on the next supply flight. We've already talked at length about the disappearance of the men, but it keeps coming up anyway. I'm halfway through dealing the first hand of our second Euchre game when Wendy asks a question.

"How do they know this mystery poop belongs to the so-called Wapa?"

"I've been wondering the same thing," Rachael adds. "If none of them have ever seen one, how would they have any idea?"

"I talked to Babuta and he explained it like this," Jeff says. "None of the living Kilo have ever seen a Wapa. The best they have is a description from previous generations, but no confirmed sightings. They don't even know what Wapa poop looks like. At least, not until today."

"Wait," I cut in. "You're telling me that not only have the Kilo never seen an actual Wapa, they've never even seen the poop they're so excited about either?"

"Crazy, I know, but that's what Babuta told me."

"So how do they know it was from a Wapa? How do they know they're not just out on a wild goose chase?"

"According to Babuta, the way Henry and the others could be so sure was because they know exactly what every other type of animal poop looks like. When they see one they don't know, it must be the Wapa." Jeff delivers this little report with confidence, something the rest of us don't seem to share. Babuta is an older woman from the tribe. Not old enough to be a member of the Biddies, but close.

"I guess it makes sense," Rachael says. "But if I were them I'd want more than a good guess."

"Yeah, me too. But think about it from their perspective," Wendy adds. "Village life isn't exactly exciting and this livens things up. If there was a once-in-a-lifetime chance to see something cool, would you be willing to risk a little camping trip to see it?"

"I see what you're saying, but it still seems a bit shady. Camping in the jungle is no picnic at the park."

The rest of the evening proceeds along similar lines. We play three games of Euchre but Rachael probably wouldn't want me to tell you the results. We play husbands against wives for the first two and the men win easily. For the third game we switch it up and play couples and Jeff and Wendy win by two.

We go through our Wednesday night routine of Bible reading and prayer. We make special mention of the Kilo men out in the jungle, and then Jeff and Wendy head for home. Rachael and I head to bed and eventually drift off to sleep in each other's arms.

***

A loud pounding on the front door jolts me awake. I squint at the clock on the wall and eventually see that it says 12:45 am.

I wipe my arm across my mouth and rise clumsily to my feet. I stumble to the door and throw it open, not even bothering to look through the window at who's there.

It's Deedap, Henry's son.

"There is death in the jungle!"

"Huh? Um...What? I mean....Ah...."

At the moment I can barely express half of a rational thought. You know that little hourglass icon that lets you know your computer is on but not functioning? That's my brain right about now. I struggle and stammer until I manage to eke out, "What are you talking about?"

"In the jungle...he is dying. Come quick....Help!" Deedap is also stammering, but for a different reason. He is out of breath and struggling to get complete sentences out. He has obviously been running.

"Who is dying?! And where?"

"My father...the jungle...chasing the sun."

"Henry is dead?!?!" My mind finally starts to fire on all cylinders.

"No," he replies, his breath coming easier. "Not dead. He is hurt. He will die if you do not..."

I cut him off. "Where?! What happened?!"

"He fell injured on the trail. It is bad. You must help!"

"How far?"

"One day beyond the cordaleet trees."

"How is he hurt? Did he fall?" The Kilo are notorious for being non-specific about health issues. Deedap said Henry "fell injured," which could mean anything.

"No time for questions...you must go...he will die!"

"Go get Jeff. Tell him to meet me at the airstrip."

Deedap races to wake Jeff. I turn around and there's Rachael, already pulling my backpack out of the hall closet. I reach up and pull down the medical kit

I keep there, mentally creating a list of things I need. I have no idea what has happened, only that Henry is hurt and it is serious enough to make Deedap run all the way home. (The Kilo are excellent runners with enough endurance to make a marathon runner jealous.)

I fill the bag with the emergency kit and traveling medicine pack. I head to the kitchen for water bottles, but Rachael stops me with a hand on my arm.

"You might want to think about some pants," she says with a grin and a glance downwards.

My eyes follow hers and my face flushes again. I just had an entire conversation with Deedap in my underwear! He didn't notice, and, considering the circumstances, it's irrelevant. But I'm embarrassed anyway.

"Right. Yeah," I mumble.

"Not that *I* mind," she says with another grin, "but the jungle can be uncomfortable enough, even with pants."

I seriously can't even believe this woman. Here I am, in the middle of an emergency, and she's flirting with me. I love her—she is just incredible!

A minute later I'm racing out of the bedroom and Rachael is waiting in the kitchen. She has my backpack ready to go. Inside are the first-aid box, some water, granola bars, a flashlight, survival kit, and a poncho. I sling it on over my shoulder and slip on a pair of shoes, stepping down on the backs in that way my dad used to hate when I was a kid. I stop at the door long enough to grab my shotgun, adding a box of shells to my pack. Shotguns and missionaries might not seem like a mix, but they are in the jungle.

In the yard I jump on my motorcycle and kick it

to life, roaring down the lane toward the airstrip. My mind is racing as fast as the engine. Did you ever have a moment when a dozen thoughts flash into your head at once? That's what happens to me on the way to the airstrip, where I hope Jeff is waiting.

*What happened?*
*How bad is it?*
*Is there gas in the tank?*
*Did I bring a flashlight?*
*How far away are they?*
*Why have they been gone so long?*

When I reach the airway, I throttle down and skid to a stop next to Jeff, dust billowing through the glow of our headlamps. He has a pack just like mine, but no shotgun. Mine is riding alongside in a scabbard like a cowboy's. At least, that's how I think of it. I rigged it up myself and it works like the ones made for horses. It keeps the gun tucked against the bike and away from trail branches, but still within reach. I offered to make one for Jeff but he declined. Something about looking silly. As if there was anyone in the jungle who would care. Whatever. Right now we've got bigger things to worry about.

"Where's Deedap?" I shout over the engines.

"He said he can't go with us. He ran all the way back to the village, and he's exhausted."

"How are we supposed to find them?"

"From the air strip, take the trail west until it ends. After that just follow the tracks. He said they continue to the west."

"That's all he gave us to go on?!"

"They have at least two dozen guys—the trail

shouldn't be hard to find."

He's right. Even Kilo hunters can't walk in a group of twenty guys and not leave a trail.

"Yeah, but I wish we knew more."

"Come on," he teases, "I thought you were a Jungle Missionary. John Wayne meets Hudson Taylor and all that?"

In spite of the tension, I grin and do my best impression of the Duke. "Well, then, saddle up, Pilgrim. We're burning daylight."

Before Jeff can point out there's no daylight at 1:00 am, I gun the motor and take off. He quickly follows and his headlamp throws shadows onto the ground in front of me. Jeff follows at a comfortable distance as we make our way quickly over the airstrip. He's close enough to stay with me, but far enough away that he's not choking on dust and exhaust.

The trail to the cordaleet trees is well-worn and well-known. The village travels it every five months during the harvest. I slow down and point the bike's headlight onto the trail, where I easily pick up the tracks of the hunting party. There has been no rain, so they are easy to follow. I click on the hi-beam and gun the motor, instantly picking up speed. Originally designed for off-road racing, the Yamahas are perfect for the jungle. With oversized shocks and knobby tires, they make excellent trail bikes.

I remember the day when we first got the bikes operational. They had arrived on the plane, one a time, and we waited until both arrived so we could assemble them together. The process took a few months and when we were done the Kilo were scared to death.

Imagine being a jungle tribesman who has never seen a motorbike. After the shock wore off and they stopped being afraid (except that one guy I told you about who kept hiding mine in the jungle), the Kilo christened the bikes "ground planes."

The trail was cut well, but it's in need of some maintenance. It's fine for walking, but you don't need a wide trail to walk down. Riding a motorcycle, however, is a different story. When we first arrived, Jeff and I paid some of the young men in the tribe to widen the trail so we could ride the bikes on it. Since then the jungle has reclaimed the edges. Branches and leaves slap at my hands and arms as I whip along, but I'm not slowing down.

I have no idea what's wrong with Henry, only that it's serious. And anything that puts Henry in serious condition puts us all in serious condition. Henry has become indispensable to the work here. I don't even want to think about how far back the goal of Bible translation would be set without him. Years at least, and those will be years we cannot afford to lose. More than that, those are years the Kilo cannot afford for us to lose. The thought of that many more Kilo dying before they can ever hear God's Word in their own language is something too terrible to contemplate. I start to panic as the ramifications of losing Henry hit me.

But I can't think about all that right now or I'll lose it for sure. I need to focus.

I try to concentrate on what I know. Deedap said they were "one day beyond the cordaleet." That is two days beyond the village, so the hunting party is a three-day walk away.

The Kilo typically walk eight miles a day, max. That might not sound like much, but keep in mind—these are barefooted people walking jungle trails. Usually while carrying children, baskets of fruit, and firewood. So Jeff and I have many miles to cover before we reach the hunting party. In the dark. It's going to be a long ride.

## Chapter 6

We pull to a stop at the cordaleet trees. I have no idea how long we have been riding, but it feels like forever. Jungle riding is no Sunday drive. I glance down and see stray leaves and twigs stuck to the tires. Some lodged in the wheels. My hands are nicked up, but nothing serious. Mostly I'm just sore. My shoulders ache and my hands are trembling from the tension of gripping the handlebars. I read one time that a good rider stays "loose in the arms." Whoever said that probably never rode in the jungle.

We nudge the bikes over to the shelter, a lean-to with three walls and a roof where the Kilo stay during the harvest. The headlamps cast an eerie glow around the clearing, revealing the first ring of cordaleet trees at the edge. Judging by the size of the fruit, I would estimate the harvest is about a month away. That means the fruit is inedible at this point, not even worth the effort to pick it. Which is fine because I have no appetite.

"I'll fill the tanks, you find the trail," Jeff says as we park the bikes and kill the motors.

"Where did Deedap say the trail was?"

"He said to go west and 'a day past the cordaleet.'"

"Right. So we're looking for a trail that goes west."

Even as I say it I am aware of the irritation in my voice. The urgency and enthusiasm we set out with has burned off and frustration is taking its place. I'm frustrated with the vague directions. There are probably four different trails that go west in this part of the jungle. I'm frustrated with the lack of clarity in the Kilo language, and I'm frustrated at my ongoing ignorance in this whole situation. More than anything else, though, I am frustrated by my own lousy attitude. It's probably a good thing our supporters can't see me right now, but then again, maybe that wouldn't be all bad. Missionaries are sinners too, and if they knew how much I struggled spiritually it might spur them on to pray for the work more.

Jeff takes off walking the perimeter of the camp, searching for the west trail, while I go for the gas cans. We keep two of them here, in a small shed behind the shelter. The Kilo have no need of gas, but we come here often enough that it makes sense to store some, just in case. The containers are plastic (anything metal left in the jungle wouldn't last two months without rusting out) and hold four gallons each.

Holding the flashlight in my teeth, I unscrew the cap on the gas tank of Jeff's bike and hoist up the first can. The tank is half full, so it won't take the entire four gallons, which is good, because we'll need some for the return trip. I top it off, careful not to spill any onto the motor. I have no idea if a motorcycle engine gets hot enough to ignite gasoline, and I have no desire to find out the hard way.

As I screw the cap on, I see Jeff coming back, his flashlight illuminating the ground as he walks. He fills me in as I fill the tank.

"The trail is just over there," he says, indicating the way he came.

"How much of a trail is it?"

"Not much. But it could be worse."

The bikes roar to life as we kick the starters and take off. This time I follow Jeff because he knows where the trail is. It takes about a minute to pick our way across the clearing, and the total time we were stopped was less than five minutes. Not exactly a NASCAR-worthy pit stop, but not bad for two amateurs.

Jeff slows as we approach an opening in the brush, then noses his bike onto the trail. I hesitate a second or two to give him some lead time, then follow. The contrast of the trail we just entered and the trail we left is immediately apparent. The jungle is encroaching on both sides and the vines hang down from above, almost touching my head as I stand on the pegs. Even from my position behind Jeff I can see that forward visibility is only about twenty yards. This forces us to slow down and stretches out our travel time.

The decreased pace isn't all bad, though. It allows me more time to think, rather than just react. I do my best to dodge and weave around branches, but I'm not always successful. The branches slash at my hands and within minutes I'm bleeding from several scrapes. Occasionally, vines get snagged on the handlebars or the hand brake, and when they do the bike starts to jerk and nose-dive forward, but fortunately lets up when the vines snap and are left swirling in the dust cloud kicked up to my rear. At one point I almost lose control, however, and for a terrifying second I contemplate the taste of tree bark before righting the bike on the trail. I see Jeff throw a quick glance backwards—he must have seen my light bobbing and jerking. But I don't stop and neither does he. We are plowing ahead toward whatever waits for us, with the hunting party somewhere up ahead.

I'm kicking myself for not grabbing my watch when I left the house. The bikes are designed for trail riding and have no speedometer. There's an odometer, but I didn't note the mileage before we left. I have no idea how far we've ridden, how long it has taken us, how fast we've been going, or even what time it is. I'm hoping Jeff has a watch but I'll have to wait until we stop again to find out. For now I keep my shoulders down and my head up as we navigate the trail ahead.

It's probably been less than an hour, but it feels like a lot more. I don't remember much from science class (other than the seventeen pencil holes in the ceiling tile above my desk), but I do remember something about time being relative. I have no idea how that works, but it seems to be true. The good times always go by quick and the bad times seem to last forever. That's me right now. My shoulders ache. My head is pounding. The insides of my legs feel like they are burning from the heat of the engine and my hands are numb and bleeding from a half-dozen small cuts. I'm just starting to feel really miserable when I almost collide with Jeff.

We round a tight corner of the trail and I'm beginning to accelerate back up to speed when he jams on his brakes, stopping dead in the middle of the trail. I hit the brakes, lock up the wheels, and skid to a stop beside him, my right leg buried in the brush. Our headlamps glow together in the darkness, illuminating the scene in front of us.

There are Kilo scattered across a clearing, sprawled in hammocks slung from trees with a few spread out on the ground. The clearing is newly made and obviously a rush job. Stumps and rocks litter the ground. Piles of branches have been shoved off to the side. Small fires are scattered around, the air thick with smoke. The fires aren't actually burning much, more like smoldering. A quick glance tells me what happened: the hunting party stopped for the night and cleared a spot to camp. The fires were kindled and before bed the hot coals were covered with green branches. The result is a slow smolder that produces lots of smoke. The smoke acts as a mosquito deterrent, keeping the bugs away so the men can sleep. It's an old jungle trick. Hard on the lungs, but easier on the skin than swatting mosquitos all night in your sleep.

We sit side-by-side and take in what we can make out in the smoky gloom of our headlamps. The dust we kicked up rolls through the small camp as a few heads poke up and sleeping men roll over, startled by the intrusion of sound and light.

I am about to turn and ask Jeff what he thinks we ought to do now, when a young man I recognize approaches us.

His name is Kanteel and he is among the youngest men in the tribe. The Kilo don't have a strict social system of rank but, generally speaking, the older you are the more status you have.

"What happened?" I ask him.

"Mahala fell injured."

"I know, but how?"

"Come and see." With that he turns to leave. First Deedap, and now this. What is it with these guys not wanting to tell me what's going on? Needless to say, I am not comforted by the responses I keep getting.

We leave the bikes, doing the best we can to prop them on the kickstands in the soft earth. We douse the headlamps and the jungle is plunged into darkness. The glow of the smoldering fires is just barely enough to see by. We pick our way slowly along, careful to step around the men sprawled in the clearing. We follow around to the back of a large tree and I can just make out a single hammock slung there.

Jeff and I click on our flashlights almost simultaneously. Kanteel was unprepared for the sudden brightness and he turns away from the light with a grimace. I imagine that must be what I looked like just a couple hours ago when Deedap tried to pound down my door.

We take two steps around the tree and approach the hammock, training the beams of our flashlights down into its folds. A jungle hammock is completely unlike the typical ones back home. It is made of small, twine-like fibers, knitted together in such a way that gives it more strength than you would ever figure when you see it for the first time. A person lays down diagonally and the resulting posture is almost flat, with your head lolling to the side slightly. As we peel back the side of the hammock, we bathe Henry's face in light and I am both sickened and saddened by what I see.

It's not pretty.

Henry is lying in the hammock, apparently asleep, and he looks terrible. His face is a mass of red welts— clear evidence of mosquito feasting—and his right temple is matted with blood. He doesn't even stir as I shine my light into his face, not even the involuntary squint and grimace of a sleeping set of eyes suddenly met with light.

"What happened?" I ask.

"He was delirious. Crazy talk. I make him sleep."

"You did what?" I have no idea what Kanteel is talking about, but apparently Jeff does.

"He knocked him out," he says flatly.

I pause, not knowing what to say. "He looks…."

"Dead," Jeff finishes.

He's right. Henry looks dead.

## Chapter 7

If it wasn't for the rise and fall of his chest, we would have thought Henry really was dead. His skin is marked by welts from the mosquitos, matted blood has started to congeal along the side of his head, and his whole body is limp. Not the relaxed kind of limp you see in a sleeping person, but the totally slack limp of a body without life.

"You knocked him out?!" I practically shouted at Kanteel. "Why?"

"He was becoming crazy. So I make him sleep."

"You could have hurt him—you could have killed him!"

"Ian! Chill. We weren't here, we've got no idea what went on." Jeff is trying to calm me down and it works. If only because I'm embarrassed at losing my cool.

"Yeah, okay, you're right," I say, trying to wrap my head around things.

At this point we still have no idea what actually happened to Henry. All we know is he was injured, he might die, he was becoming delirious, so Kanteel knocked him out to keep him quiet and still. In the two or three seconds it takes me to assess things I realize I might have done the same thing if I were he. No doubt Kanteel was stuck looking after Henry while the rest of the men went to sleep for the night, he being the youngest and all. The older guys pulled rank and left him to deal with an unstable man who was bigger than he was. When I think about it like that, I can't fault him for what he did.

Now that we've all calmed down (okay, okay, now that *I've* calmed down), maybe we can figure out exactly what happened.

"What happened before," I ask, "when Henry was hurt?"

"Better to show," Kanteel says, taking the light from Jeff.

Again with the not answering my questions. What is up with these guys?

He moves two small steps toward the foot of the hammock, letting the part near Henry's head close up over his face. The light sweeps the length of his body as Kanteel pulls back the edge of the hammock and retreats a half step.

"You look," he says, with the hesitancy of a young man giving instructions to an older man.

His words come out more like a question, the imaginary question mark stuck on the end like a stow-away. As Kanteel holds back the edge of the hammock, I lift up a loose piece of material that has been wrapped around Henry's foot and lower leg. It's a crude excuse for a bandage, but not bad considering the Kilo rarely have excess cloth to begin with.

As soon as I see the bandage I know something bad is coming. The dark stain doesn't cover the whole thing, but it comes close. The unmistakable scent of blood wafts up from Henry's foot as Jeff and I lean over to peer at his wound. The entire top of his foot is covered in blood. Part of the skin seems to have been scraped off, exposing the tissue underneath. I'm pretty sure I can see bone in one place, but the combination of smoke and the flicker of a dying flashlight beam make my initial impression unreliable. Jeff takes his light back from Kanteel and trains it onto Henry's foot along with mine. Through the concentrated light of the two beams we notice that the cut on the top of Henry's foot is the least of his worries. His big toe is nearly gone!

Not gone as in disappeared. Gone as in hacked off. From what I can see through the haze, his big toe is, literally, hanging by a thread. It appears that someone, or something, cut through his big toe on a slight angle, stopping just short of slicing the whole thing off. The skin on the bottom of his toe is still intact, but that's it. The rest of it, bone and all, has been severed, right at the joint. The toe is lolled off to the side—gruesome, to say the least.

No wonder he was getting delirious. Henry must have been in excruciating pain, enough to drive anyone crazy. He's a tough guy, but everyone has their limits. More than one time we have heard stories of Kilo being seriously injured in freak accidents and choosing to kill themselves, or have their friends kill them, rather than suffer the ongoing pain of a severe injury. It is an appalling practice and, thankfully, hasn't happened during our time here. But in the absence of painkillers, I can understand the desire to end suffering. Given the alternative, maybe Kanteel knocking him out was an act of mercy.

"Oh my gosh!" I spew out the words in a rush, articulate as always. Jeff isn't much better than me.

"That's bad, Ian. Really bad."

"When did this happen?" I ask, noticing that small flies and ants are starting to appear on the bandage, and also the edges of Henry's foot, no doubt attracted to the wound by the scent of the blood. I turn away from the hammock, afraid I might vomit.

"Before today," Kanteel tells us. This is the typical Kilo phrase for "yesterday." "We searched all day but found no Wapa. When it was dark Mahala says we must stop. We clear trees and set the camp. Mahala watched all, until it came time to sleep. He came to the tree to hang his hammock. I was not here. I did not see."

"How did he get his foot cut off hanging a hammock?" Jeff asks.

"There were three other men, all hanging hammocks." At this he points to the other side of the tree where I remember making my way around the three guys he is talking about.

"One of them sees a snake on the tree in the dark and makes to kill it with his machete. The snake was not a snake. It was the vine from Mahala's hammock. He was holding it with a foot while he pulled the hammock up to the branch. The machete…"

He stops talking but makes a slicing motion with his hand, like a karate chop through the air. Then he continues.

"It cut him."

I'm stunned. Several things in this story seem to lack credibility. First of all, how many times has Henry hung up hammocks in the jungle with these guys? Hundreds? At least. This has never happened before.

Second, why would somebody think there was

a snake? There are no snakes here. I've been here for two years and have yet to see a snake. These guys know there are no snakes. So what was this guy so freaked out about that he would not only think he saw a snake, but also try and slice through it so fast he didn't realize Henry's foot was there?

"But there are no snakes here," I protest. "Why did he think there was a snake?"

"The Wapa always come with the snakes."

"The story," Jeff interjects. "From Supato. She said the Wapa always come with snakes when they return east"

Immediately, I recall my conversation with Supato from Monday morning. She explained to me that, according to legend, whenever a Wapa returns east to reclaim their homeland from the Kilo, they enlist the help of snakes to frighten the people into running. The guy who slashed Henry's toe overreacted because he was terrified by this legend.

If this were a cartoon, a light bulb would have lit up above my head, because it all suddenly clicked into place. The guy who cut Henry had spent his whole life listening to the legends about the Wapa, and the snakes that return with them. He had just spent two days hunting for Wapa, following a trail, knowing that where there was a Wapa, there had to be poisonous snakes.

So there he is, setting up camp in the near-dark of a smoke-filled jungle camp after sunset. He goes to hang his hammock, looks down, sees a snake on the ground next to the tree, and he about jumps out of his skin. In a flash he has his machete out and is slicing through the air toward the snake. He's going to be a hero!

Too late, he realizes it's not a snake. He tries to alter the path of his machete but physics are physics. He knows nothing about physics, of course, but a second later Henry knows all about pain. Henry must have been slightly up the tree, his feet grasping the bark in a downward grip of the toes in that weird way only Kilo can climb trees. The machete scraped along the top of his foot, exposing the flesh underneath, before practically severing his toe.

I look around, flashing my light toward the tree. Sure enough, there's a fresh gash in the bark and a section of rope-vine lying on the ground at the base of the tree.

"What now?" I ask, mostly to myself.

"We've got a kit," Jeff says. "Fix him up."

"Fix him up? He doesn't need a bandage, he needs surgery."

"Do you see any surgeons around here? Ian, it's just you and me."

"Yeah, but what are we gonna do with this?" I ask, gesturing down at Henry's flayed foot and hanging toe. "It's not like we can sew it back on."

"Why not?"

"*Are you nuts?!* We're not surgeons!"

"What other choice do we have, Ian? Besides, you've sewed up lots of people remember?"

I'm not a medic. Not in the traditional sense. I do know first aid, but that's not even remotely close to the same thing. Every team of tribal missionaries sent into the jungle receives basic training in first-aid and emergency medical treatment. When the nearest doctor is a two-hour flight away, you can't run to Urgent Care for every little cut and bruise. Ditto for bigger stuff. Because of this, every jungle missionary can tape ankles, deal with burns, splint up dislocated fingers, even diagnose and treat concussions. And Jeff is right. I *have* sewn up a few cuts. It's not a required part of the training, but the mission expects at least one person on each team to be able to suture a wound without puking. Like I said, the doctor is hours away.

But this is not a minor wound. This is a severed toe. As in cut off. All the way. Through the joint and everything. There is no way. I start shaking my head, but Jeff breaks in.

"Ian—what have we got to lose?"

"For starters? His foot! I can't even begin to tell you how wrong this could go. What about the nerves? The ligaments? I can do stitches, but not tendons. What about infection? What if I screw it up and he dies? If we lose Henry we'll have an even bigger problem on our hands." I'm practically shouting at this point and it takes a physical effort to bring myself under control.

"I get all that," Jeff says. "And you don't have to tell me how important Henry is here. But if we do nothing it'll get infected for sure. If we try something we'll at least have a chance. Like I said, what have we got to lose? It's not like you can mess it up worse than it already is. It's like the vacuum cleaner all over again."

The vacuum cleaner.

My mind flashes back to our third year of Missions training. Rachael and I had been married for six months. Jeff and Wendy for nine. No one supports missionaries in training, only missionaries in the field, so we were poor. I was working part-time and going to school full-time. Ditto for Jeff. Rachael worked as a nanny and part-time campus secretary. We were living in campus housing, eating in the cafeteria to save money, and sharing a bathroom down the hall. With another married couple, plus Jeff and Wendy. Three couples, one bathroom. Beyond poor. I heard through the grapevine that they don't do it that way on campus any more. Someone came to their senses and got everyone their own bathrooms. Must be nice.

I came home from work one day to a broken vacuum. It had just stopped working. There was a sharp acrid smell, a little smoke, and a whole lot of nothing in the way of suction. I came through the door and there it was, propped in the living/dining/entryway room (it was a very small apartment), smelling like a dead animal that needs to go out with the trash. Which is exactly what a normal person would have done—throw it away. But we were not normal people. We were sharing a bathroom and a vacuum with two other couples. We were poor. We couldn't afford a new vacuum cleaner.

"I'll fix it," I announced that day.

Did I have any idea how to fix a vacuum cleaner? Of course not. I knew nothing about vacuum cleaners, but it was already broke, right? It's not like I could break it worse than it was already broken. I took it apart piece by piece, lining up the pieces on the table, careful not to lose any of them. I kept going until I found something that looked broke. There was a charred-looking wire and a half-melted piece of plastic. I had no idea what those parts were, but I could tell they weren't going to work the way they were supposed to. Not anymore.

I snapped off the melted plastic and shunted in a replacement piece that I carved from a plastic plate that was about the same thickness (no, I'm not kidding), setting it in place somehow. Superglue, I think. The wire didn't seem to be connected to anything, so I pulled it out and then I reassembled the whole thing. Going in reverse order, one piece at a time. When I was done I had five parts left over.

We held our breath as I plugged it in, fully expecting to get zapped and maybe start a fire. Nothing happened. No zap. No fire. We took a breath and Rachael turned it on. It fired right up and actually worked. I don't know how and I don't know why. But it worked. Rachael swore it worked even better than before, but I think she was just being nice. I kept those extra parts, just in case. Eventually I threw them out when it became apparent the crazy thing was good to go for real.

I look up at Jeff and I can't believe this is happening. He's grinning and the haze of the fire and the diffused light of the flashlights make him look almost manic, like a mad scientist. Like we're about to do something insane. Which we are. I'm about to try to sew on a severed toe.

"Like the vacuum cleaner," I say (and to myself, *Yeah, sure…*).

"Just like it," Jeff replies with a confidence I am not sharing.

"Okay, fine, I'll do it," I say, giving in.

***

Step One, even in the jungle: stabilize the patient. We pick up Henry, the three of us together. I grab his injured leg and hold him with one hand under his knee, the other under his thigh. Jeff hooks his hands under Henry's armpits and Kanteel grabs his other leg. We gently wrestle Henry to the ground and lay him flat. He's still out cold. Kanteel must have hit him hard. That is probably a good thing, because this is not going to be pleasant.

Once we've lain him on the ground we stretch out his legs, careful to keep the dirt out of the bandage and the stress off of his foot. Jeff takes out an emergency poncho and we get it arranged under the lower half of Henry's body. It's a poor excuse for an operating table, but it's all we've got.

Step Two: try to establish some sort of sterile environment. We flood Henry's lower leg, foot, and toes with alcohol—sterilization the Old School way. If he was awake he'd no doubt be howling from the sting. That would be the least of his worries.

Step Three: have a plan. Which I don't.

"Got any bright ideas on how this should go?" I look across at Jeff, who's kneeling on the other side.

"Yeah," he says, that crazy grin back on his face. "Point the nail up."

"The nail?" I start to say, not understanding. "What are you…" And then it hits me. "Oh. Right. Thanks for that."

"Hey, you asked." That grin again. First my wife, now Jeff. Everyone in my life is a comedian.

With the tension of the moment broken, I relax a little and start to work. In reality it's a pretty straight-forward process. I flood the wound with more alcohol. I read one time that using alcohol to sterilize wounds can actually damage the tissue and slow the healing process. I'm not a betting man, but if I was, I'd bet that whoever wrote that article never sewed up anyone in the jungle. I'd also bet that jungle germs can do way more damage than a little alcohol, so onto the wound it goes. If a little is good, a lot is better, right?

Yeah, we'll go with that.

If this was a real surgery I'm sure there would be all kinds of elaborate procedures to follow. Identify nerves and blood vessels. Scan for this, test for that. Prepare for transfusions or some other such thing, but we have none of that here. What we have is me, missionary turned jungle medic. We have Jeff, holding a flashlight with one hand and Henry's leg with the other. We have an emergency kit with basic supplies. I've got Henry's big toe in one hand, looking like a horror-movie prop, and I've got the suture needle threaded up and ready to go. Jeff reaches across from the other side of Henry and gently bends his leg at the knee, flattening out his foot, making the angle a bit easier on me.

From there it's basic stitches, only in a circle. I start at the bottom of his foot and work my way around his toe, toward myself. The basic technique of stitches is always the same: in one side, out the other. Pull tight and repeat. So that's what I do. In one side and out the other, over and over again. Halfway through the process the flashlight flickers—exactly what we didn't need. Jeff hits it against the side of his leg, which does nothing.

"Needs batteries," I say, ever the observant one.

Batteries are notorious in the jungle. The heat and humidity rot them out and they fail at a rate almost double what they would back home. We try and compensate by keeping them sealed up in plastic containers, but decay is inevitable. Jeff lets go of Henry's leg to deal with the flashlight, and the sudden change in angle causes two of my stitches to pop. This does not engender confidence in me and I have another momentary attack of doubt. Are we seriously going to go through with this? But it's too late to turn back now.

It takes Jeff a full minute to get the fresh batteries opened and installed in his light. During this time Henry begins to stir. I've always wondered if unconscious people can feel pain, and this has got to be pushing the limits. His moans become more pronounced and he is starting to fidget a bit. He is obviously coming to. This is not good.

Kanteel makes like he's going to hit Henry again, but Jeff puts up a hand.

"Hold on," he says, turning back to his pack. He pulls out a plastic box with two clips on it to keep it sealed shut, and a heavy-duty rubber seal. It's painted a dull green. Army green.

"Picked this up from a guy selling surplus. I didn't really have a use for it, but for two dollars I couldn't pass it up."

"What is it?" I ask, not really giving him a chance to answer before asking again, "And isn't buying military surplus illegal?"

"It's an army medic field kit, and the guy told me

it's top notch. Military grade, but not military issue. It's for First Responders and people like that. Apparently there's a difference."

"So says the guy selling 'top notch' kits on the street for two dollars. It's probably stolen."

"Whatever. Nimishish. What's important is we have it. And you'll never guess what's in it." He holds up a bottle with a caution label almost as big as the bottle itself. There's a line of Spanish writing underneath and even though I don't recognize a lot of the words themselves, I get the basic idea.

"Is that chloroform?" I blurt out.

"Yep. Military grade, supposedly."

"You've got to be kidding me," I mumble as Jeff tucks his nose inside his shirt in preparation for opening the bottle.

I do likewise, getting a good whiff of myself in the process. It's not a pretty scent. I have to let go of Henry's foot with one hand for a split second, which brings on a whole new round of moans and fidgeting. Jeff douses the rag that came with the bottle and gently places it over Henry's mouth and nose. In three seconds he's still again. We double-check to make sure he's still breathing, and then Jeff trains his light back down toward the foot-end of things.

"I've always wanted to do that," he says. "Just like the Hardy Boys."

"No," I reply. "In The Hardy Boys it was always the bad guys who had chloroform."

The rest of the operation (if you can call it that) goes smoothly. Almost perfectly. The angle of things makes the last few stitches a bit more difficult, but by then the rest of the toe is more or less attached, which allows me to work directly with two hands. I eventually finish the last suture, tie off the string, and snip it down close to Henry's foot. Picking up my light from where it was propped on the poncho, I survey my handiwork. It is not pretty. Predictably, Jeff thinks everything is just great.

"Not bad," he says, ever the optimist.

"Are you kidding me? Even Dr. Frankenstein would be embarrassed by this."

"Well it's not terrible," he replies—his favorite line for when he doesn't want to admit disaster. "It could have gone worse."

"It can always get worse."

"That's my point. We're lucky and you should count your blessings. And if I ever see the guy who sold me that kit, I'm gonna hug him."

"You're a lunatic, you know that, right?"

"All the good people are, Ian. All the good people are."

Henry begins to stir. He moans and tries to fidget but he's still mostly unconscious. While he's still out, we pour more alcohol over the fresh sutures. We wrap it up in gauze and bandages from the kit, adding a healthy smear of antibiotic cream all the way around. As soon as that's done and the wound is officially closed, I can suddenly feel the tension and pressure I'd been working so hard to ignore.

My head slumps and my shoulders tense. The headache is immediate and my hands start to shake as the adrenaline rush ebbs. I reach for that life-saving first-aid kit, the one probably purchased illegally with a bottle of chloroform inside. I fumble around, searching for aspirin, but find a blister pack full of one-time-use syringes instead. Pulling them out, I can't believe what I'm seeing.

"Are these morphine?" I ask, not sure if I'm hoping for a positive or a negative answer.

"Yep," Jeff replies, trying way too hard to sound casual and hide his smile. "You threw such a fit about the chloroform, I didn't want to bring it up before. I figure Henry's going to be *really* grateful for those little guys when he wakes up."

"Yeah, until he gets addicted," I say. "This is great. We're gonna turn the most important member of our translation team into an addict. Fantastic."

But even as I say it I know how petty I sound. Right now any kind of pain killers are a godsend for Henry. Besides, there's only six syringes in the pack, not nearly enough to cause an addiction. I hope. Probably not even enough to get him through the worst of what's coming, but better than nothing.

Jeff starts to laugh and even though it seems absurd in the moment, I'm soon laughing along with him.

"Can you believe this?" he asks. "We just sewed a toe back on in the middle of the night, in a jungle camp. This is going to make one whopper of an opener!"

He's right. Forever and all time, no matter what happens, this one will be the story we tell when we speak to groups. Especially youth groups. Adult groups ask boring questions about support levels and that sort of thing. The kids always want stories. Jungle adventures, tribal life, stuff like that. The weirder, the better, and they don't get much weirder than what we just did, that's for sure.

Henry stirs again and I look down at my friend. His toe is wrapped up tight and we're hoping the little bit of pressure from the wrap will help hold the stitches in place. Whether or not the stitches take and his toe survives is out of our hands. It will take a miracle.

Then again, every missionary can tell you stories about miracles. Since going to the mission field I have realized that, back home, people have a pretty low threshold for what they consider miraculous. When your life is as comfortable as life has become for everyone in today's America, you tend to openly marvel when even moderately difficult things go your way. In the jungle we just call that life.

Life is good here, but it's not always easy. If his toe makes it, it will be a miracle, but my concern lies chiefly with his foot. The real fight will be from infection in Henry's foot. He's got a section of skin about an inch-and-a-half wide and three or four inches long that was basically flayed off. Nothing we can do. We loaded it with antibiotic ointment, wrapped the whole thing up, and prayed for the best.

With some difficulty, being cautious not to bump his foot, we get Henry back into the hammock. He almost wakes up and just as I'm thinking about giving him a shot of morphine, he drifts back into sleep. I have no idea how long chloroform keeps you knocked out, but I'm hoping for the best.

Jeff didn't bring a watch either, but time doesn't really matter right now anyway. We're not going anywhere for a while. For the time being, whatever time it is, we are where we'll be.

How's that for philosophical?

Dawn hasn't started to break yet, so Jeff and I tell Kanteel to get some sleep. He's unsure at first, afraid he'll get in trouble for abandoning his post. I tell him it's okay, I'll make sure Henry is fine, and after that he doesn't hang around any longer.

I take the first watch, not that we can tell when it's time to swap or anything like that. As Jeff settles back against the tree and tries to get comfortable, I balance the shotgun across my outstretched knees and say a silent prayer. We hear about jaguars way more than anyone actually sees them. Even still, it would be foolish to pretend they didn't exist, or that they weren't out there in the darkness somewhere. The shotgun is probably unnecessary, but it makes me feel better.

I have yet to see a jaguar in the wild here, let alone have reason to shoot one. At this point the only thing my shotgun has killed has been a few wild pigs and a rodent-groundhog-looking thing that was digging in my garden. I don't keep a shell in the chamber, but it's nice to know that a dead jaguar is only a quick pump and aim away. If I can actually hit it, that is.

I lean back against the tree and feel my body begin to relax. I'll fall asleep thinking about what just happened. It was easily the grossest but coolest thing I have ever done. For the first time I'm actually starting to feel a little like Indiana Jones—almost.

## Chapter 8

My eyes crack open as I hear Henry begin to stir. The fire has smoldered down to nothing and the mosquitos are having a feast on the back of my neck. I slap them away and try to sit up straight. I have no idea how long I was sleeping, but long enough that my back is protesting and clearly wants me to move. I have a pounding headache that wasn't there when I fell asleep. But despite the pain, I'm not worried. It's not like I'm sick, it's just that I haven't had any coffee in almost 24 hours and my body is screaming for some caffeine. If I was a more spiritual missionary, this probably wouldn't be a problem.

Whatever. I don't want to think about that right now. I just want some coffee.

Since there is none to be had, I suck it up and glance around to take in my surroundings. The blackness of night has been replaced by something else. Not the white light of day, or even the gray dawn of morning. Just a slightly less deep shade of black. It's almost morning, but not quite.

Henry is moaning, trying to move in the hammock. He's not having much success. Jungle hammocks are great, unless you want to move. Jeff lurches, not even half awake yet, almost bumping the gun off my lap. He must have managed to fall deeply asleep. The kind of asleep where you lose muscle tension, like when your head snaps back in church and you jerk it forward way too fast, alerting everyone that you were sleeping in church. Not that I know anyone who has ever done that.

"Wha… what happened?" Jeff asks, his voice thick with confusion.

"You fell asleep during prayer." I whisper. "We're getting ready for the closing hymn, number 352."

Okay, so it's more of a stage whisper than an actual whisper. Dumb, I know, but still funny. At least to me. Henry is trying to move around and I'm worried about his stitches. I stand up and help Jeff to his feet.

"Come on, let's see about Henry. I think he's waking up."

Henry is indeed awake now and, by the looks of him, not happy about it. His eyes are open but vacant. The phrase "lights on but nobody home" springs to mind. He is attempting to move his arms, but they don't seem to be cooperating.

"Ister eighbor? Isth at choo?"

His speech is slurred and broken, like some absurd combination of drunkenness and inner-city slang. Which is funny, because Henry has never seen a city and never tasted alcohol.

"Yeah, Henry," I reply. "It's me."

"Whaa appen?

That Henry is speaking English at all is remarkable. I can pretty much promise you that if you chopped off my toe, knocked me out, drugged me, sewed it back on, and woke me up, there is a zero percent chance I would be speaking Kilo. In that moment I am reminded how the assumptions most people have about jungle tribes are so wrong. People assume that because they don't have computers and cars and such, they must be unintelligent. As if it's stupidity that holds their society back.

In reality, Henry is one of the most intelligent people I know. His natural aptitude for language has sped up our translation process by incalculable degrees. English is his second language, but he doesn't miss much and it never takes him long to learn. He speaks more English than anyone in the village and his English proficiency far outstrips my Kilo. I wish I were half as smart as he is.

"You were hurt," I remind him. "Last night, camp set up. Do you remember?"

"I do not think I will ever forget."

"You were cut by a man trying to kill a snake, but he missed and got your toe."

"There are no snakes in this jungle. The snakes live in the West and the South."

"The snakes came with the Wapa, remember?" I realize I am telling him all of this as if I actually believe it. But I don't know what to believe at this point.

"Wapa?"

Clearly his memory isn't everything it should be yet. I have no idea what the effects of chloroform on the brain are. I only know what I read in the old Hardy Boys books about shady crooks and kidnappers who would drug people with chloroform and drive them to a remote location in the trunk of an old sedan. In the books, however, the kidnapped guy always woke up, overheard the master plan, and got rescued by the heroes. No one ever lost a toe. I like those stories better than this one.

"Yes, Henry, Wapa. You were on a hunt for Wapa; you stopped for the night, went to hang your hammock and were cut by a man who thought he saw a snake in the dark. Deedap ran to get me and we tried to fix your toe."

"Tried?"

"Yeah… tried… it's back on your foot, but I don't know if it'll stay or not." I chuckle at the words as they come out, thinking that a real doctor would never say something like that.

"I can feel it," Henry says with a grimace. "I wish I could not."

Just then Jeff walks up with his medical kit in hand.

"We can help with that," he cuts in. "I can give you something for the pain."

"Something is better than nothing." It's an old Kilo proverb about food. "And living is better than dying." Another, this one about sickness. Funny how many old sayings basically state the obvious.

Jeff kneels down and pops open the kit. He breaks the seal on a morphine syringe and re-packs everything before standing up. He hands the empty package to me and I scan the back for directions. Nothing. Just the usual jumble indicating date of manufacture and distribution. Apparently the Venezuelan Army, or whoever this kit was originally intended for, expected their medics to already know what they were doing. Imagine that.

"Nothing here about how to administer it," I point out.

"It's a syringe," Jeff says, "not that complicated. I'll do it."

He looks at Henry, tells him that it might sting a little, and with a smooth, swift motion, stabs Henry in the thigh with the syringe.

Henry's face doesn't even twitch, and he looks at Jeff and says, "Tell me when you are ready to begin."

Perfect deadpan. Not a trace of a smile or discomfort on his face. Incredible. The guy has a severed toe, the worst ER doc in the history of medicine, and a suture job that's got to be killing him. Yet here he is, ribbing Jeff like it's a schoolyard contest over who's the toughest. He wins.

Henry might be tough as nails, but even he can't hide the relief currently flooding his face. I have no idea how fast morphine is supposed to work, but in under a minute his jaw has relaxed and his eyes have softened and gone glassy. Drugs, gotta love 'em.

The jungle around us is coming to life as sunlight illuminates the camp. Men are stirring. Fires are kindled. Birds are flitting about as jaguars slink away to their lairs deep in the shadows of the forest. Okay, so maybe that last part isn't actually happening. But it sounded cool, right?

The men filter over to check on Henry. I can't figure if they're coming to give condolences or encouragement, and for the first few that look at him over the edge of the hammock, I don't think they know either. Word spreads through the camp that Henry is alive and awake, if not alert and enthusiastic, and the trickle of men soon increases to a stream. The combination of the medication, the social activity, and the exertion of simply talking is too much and Henry sinks down into the hammock as the last guy walks away. He is clearly spent and he drifts off to sleep, leaving me to ponder how often a patient can be given morphine.

Jeff has been picking up around the tree, helping take down hammocks and what-not. I look over and see him rummaging in his pack. He comes up with a couple water bottles and a handful of granola bars, tossing one of each my way. I catch the water bottle but the granola bar bounces off my thumb onto the ground. I know what's coming even before he says it, shaking his head.

"Hands like an amputee, Allen, hands like an amputee."

It's an old line, from back in the day, before anyone thought about possibly offending amputees. My brother was a football player in high school, a tailback. The story goes that in practice one day they were running a sweep play and my brother couldn't catch the pitch. After three consecutive fumbles by his star running back, the coach yelled out in frustration: "ALLEN! YOU'VE GOT HANDS LIKE AN AMPUTEE, SON! CATCH THE BALL OR I'LL TRADE YOU TO THE SOCCER TEAM FOR A WATER BOTTLE AND TWO CHEERLEADERS!!"

There were a few other words stuck in there for emphasis, but I won't repeat them now. We still laugh about it at every family Christmas and I've told the story to Jeff repeatedly. Maybe I shouldn't have.

We sit by the tree and eat quietly. All around us the camp is being torn down and the fires extinguished. The men are preparing to move on. Apparently the Wapa waits for no man, even when one of their own is missing a toe. But needless to say, Henry won't be going with them. He won't be walking anywhere for a while.

"What are we going to do with him?" Jeff asks, taking a swig of water from his bottle.

"Let him sleep, I guess. We can't move him."

"We could shoot him full of morphine and put him on the bike."

"The words *heart* and *attack* come to mind," I say, not sure if he's being serious or not. "That's what happens when you give somebody too much morphine. Their heart stops."

"You watch too many movies," Jeff replies. "Do you have any idea how much morphine it takes to stop a human heart?"

"No, do you?"

"Nope."

"Didn't think so. Better safe than sorry. Let's do one shot every six hours. Seems about right, like a hospital, you know?"

"How do you know how often a hospital gives out morphine?"

"I don't. But it sounds better than your idea."

A couple of geniuses, that's what we are.

Before the hunting party leaves, I manage to talk them into sparing a man. The old military stand-by, "rank has its privileges," is in full effect. That means the low man on the totem pole gets the shaft again. Kanteel, the young guy who met us when we first rode up to the camp, will be sent back to the village to report what has happened. This is a two-fold bummer—he will miss out on the hunt *and* it's a long run back to the village.

Before he leaves I make certain he is clear on the situation: I am not hurt. Jeff is okay. Henry is alive but his foot or leg might not make it, depending on whether my handiwork gets infected. We will be back as soon as we can move him. I don't want any misinformation causing the girls to worry. He takes off and so does the hunting party. Apparently someone just found a fresh pile of dadu, but it's the same guy who allegedly saw a snake, so we take it with a grain of salt.

Jeff is writing in his journal when I return to our camp under the tree, so I leave him alone. I can't journal. All the books and blogs talk about how therapeutic it is. I just don't get it. To me it's like running: pure torture. If someone is a runner, they can never understand how anyone could not run. But if someone isn't a runner, they can never understand how someone could enjoy running. Journaling and running—to me they both sound like torture. No thanks.

Instead I dig in my pack and find my Bible, sitting off to the side under the next tree. Devotions in the woods, just me and God, no one else around. I am now living a cliché, but I love it. For me this is one of the best things about my missionary life: devotions in the jungle whenever I want. Growing up we were always told to read our Bibles. "It's important," the adults said. "It's how you hear from God," the pastor preached. I never got it.

Until I did.

At 8th grade summer camp our counselor told us we were going to make it a daily habit. At least for one week, as long as he was our eager leader. Probably he just wanted the twenty minutes of peace and quiet he could get by sending us into the woods with our Bibles. Can't say that I blame him. "Don't talk to anyone," he said. "Don't throw rocks. Just read. You and God, alone, in the woods." A Christian cliché.

The first day was misery. I had too much of a conscience to ignore the counselor and sneak down to the waterfront like some of the other guys, but not enough attention span to actually sit and read for twenty minutes either. I kept looking at my watch, hoping twenty minutes was up. Twenty minutes felt like two days. The next day was better and I managed to read for ten minutes without looking at my watch. That might not sound like much for adults, but I'm fairly certain it set an 8th grade record at the time.

The third day I forgot I was even wearing a watch. I picked Esther at random and just started reading. I had never read it before and I got lost in the story. I actually said *Yes!* in a quiet voice when Haman got hanged on his own gallows. Not very compassionate, but like I said, I was into it. I finished Esther and read Ruth. I finished Ruth and started Job. About the time Job's friends showed up to comfort him, I heard the counselor calling my name. It had been over an hour.

I went running back to the cabin, excited over what I had read, but also embarrassed. I didn't want the other guys to think I was a Bible nerd. Stupid, but that's how junior high unfortunately works. By the time Friday rolled around, though, I didn't care. Job got boring real fast, so I started 1 Kings on Thursday and stayed out in the woods so long I almost missed dinner. Ever since then, there is just something about reading the Bible in the woods that appeals to me. Put me inside in a chair and my mind wanders after ten minutes, like I never left 8$^{th}$ grade. In the woods, though, it feels like I can read forever.

After fifteen or twenty minutes I can see Jeff put his notebook away and get out his own Bible. Don't we look like quite a picture now? Two missionaries reading their Bibles in the woods. Somebody should take a photo and mail it to our moms. They'd be so proud.

Then Henry wakes up, and not quietly either. He's moaning again and trying to move around in the hammock. Jeff and I get up and walk over, him with the medical kit and me with a bottle of water. We steady Henry in the hammock as he wakes up, but mostly we just stand there awkwardly, not sure what to do.

"Should we give him another shot?" Jeff asks.

"It's been at least six hours—that was our best guess, right?"

"Unless you've had any better ideas."

"Nope."

Henry is in obvious pain. Jeff gives him another shot of morphine, his second. The drug takes quick effect and I find myself wishing we had more. The kit came with six shots, so we have four left. As Henry's eyes register the drugs, we give him some food. He manages to eat most of a granola bar and down half a bottle of water before drifting off to sleep. I'm no expert, but I don't recall any patients on the TV medical dramas conking out this quick after every dose of a painkiller. But I was hoping the sleep would help him heal.

While I'm worrying about accidentally stopping

Henry's heart in our attempts to save his toe, Jeff says something we both should have thought of earlier.

"We should check his dressing."

"Yeah, right," I say. "Check the dressing, clean the wound, and change the bandage."

"You did the surgery—want me to take a turn?"

Jeff doesn't really wait for an answer, but starts to slowly peel back the layers of dressing wrapped around Henry's foot. The wound underneath is not pretty. We waited too long to change the bandage and the edges have started to harden with dried blood. They stick to the skin as Jeff gently pulls them away. Afraid the pain might wake Henry, I gently pour on some water to help things along.

Once the dressing is pulled back and the gauze removed, we can examine things in the light of day. Again, it is not pretty. In fact, it's just plain ugly. I know I'm not supposed to say that, and if I was a doctor I'd get low marks for bedside manner. Jeff isn't much better—in fact, he's worse.

"That looks terrible. You make a horrible surgeon, you know that?"

"Hey man, it was your idea. And besides, what did you expect from an untrained jungle doc?"

"Forget what I expected. At this point we're down to hope. As in, I hope this thing doesn't get infected. An infection puts his leg at risk and putting his leg at risk could be fatal. I know I gave you a hard time earlier, but I get it. I can't imagine finishing the translation without him. This is serious, Ian."

He has a point. A toe is one thing, and if it gets infected we can always remove the stitches and be right back where we started. A gruesome possibility, but a doable one. The real danger here is infection to his foot and leg. I don't even want to think about what blood poisoning would mean. With no other options we do our best to clean the wound, disinfect everything, apply fresh ointment, gauze, and bandages, and wrap him up again. It doesn't feel like enough, but it's all we can do.

We spend the day waiting and praying. Henry spends most of the day sleeping. The morphine has a tranquilizing effect on him, but it could be the shock and trauma as well. Without much else to do, we lapse into frequent silences, which is fine. Neither Jeff nor I have ever been the type to fill silence with small talk, so we mostly don't. But we do pray together though. We pray for Henry, for our families, and for ourselves. We pray for the Kilo hunting the Wapa. We pray for their safety and success. Which feels weird, because I'm not even certain they are actually hunting anything other than a myth. We spend the day talking through the whole situation off and on, trying to make sense of it. One exchange is typical:

"It's weird, you know?" I ask. "How do we even know there's actually something out there to hunt?"

"The only thing I know is what we've been told: Wapa scat is unlike any other droppings from any other animal around here. It's got to be something."

"Yeah, but *they* don't even know what they're hunting. They're hunting an idea. A legend that poops. How do you catch a legend?"

"Follow the poop."

"Better than the yellow brick road, I suppose."

"What if it's an endangered animal?" Jeff asks.

"What do you mean?"

"Think about it. It's supposedly an animal that used to live all over. Now it only lives in the west. It is occasionally seen, but only barely. What if it's an animal that used to be plentiful, but is now endangered?"

"You mean, what if the Wapa doesn't come around here anymore because it was overhunted?"

"Basically, yeah, that's what I'm saying."

"Could be," I say, thinking that Jeff's endangered animal theory is the best we've come up with yet.

At some point in the day he finds a deck of cards in his backpack and we play Rummy, the only two-person card game we know. It feels surreal, but it helps to pass the time.

By the time night falls Henry is awake more than he's asleep, and we fill him in on everything that happened. He wants to see his toe, but I don't think it's such a good idea. In the end I have no choice though. How do you keep a guy from looking at his own foot? When it's time to change the dressings, Jeff unwraps it and Henry takes a look. If this was a movie he would have been amazed and astounded at the incredible healing that was taking place. His foot would be half restored already and his toe looking miraculously whole.

This is not a movie.

Henry takes one look at his foot, lurches to the side, and throws up what looks like all the food he's eaten today. I just manage to get out of the way, jumping back as he turns his head and tries to lean out of the hammock.

"I am sorry," Henry manages.

"*You're* sorry?" I ask, incredulous. "Henry, you could lose your toe. A little gunk on my shoes is the least of our worries right now."

"How long have we been at this camp?" he asks us. The Kilo keep track of time based on the motion of the sun and the length of the shadow. So being under tree cover all day has left him disoriented.

"One day." I tell him. It's been twenty-four hours since he was cut, but it feels like seventy-two. Easily the longest day of my life. Not because I'm having a hard day, but because so much has happened in so little time.

"The Wapa?"

"Nothing yet. I'm sorry."

He is clearly disappointed and I wish I had a better report, but we haven't heard a thing since the men left this morning. I don't expect to.

"My wife. She will worry. I must go to her."

These short sentences are becoming an indicator of Henry's mental state. All day he has been mostly clear-headed, but whenever his sentences have gotten short like that, he's been asleep shortly after.

"Not yet," I say. "Now we need to rest. You can't move like this." I point down at his toe. It's swollen and red, but I can't tell if the redness is from infection or just a general irritation of his skin, because of the sutures. If the redness spreads, we're in trouble.

"Sleep now, Henry," Jeff adds. "We'll head for home in the morning."

Henry needs to rest if he's going to have any hope of making it home tomorrow on the bikes. Same goes for me and Jeff. In the course of our conversations today, we decided we don't have much chance but to set out for the village tomorrow. Our food is almost gone and we're down to two bottles of water. More than that, though, we're almost out of bandages for Henry. Neither of us are doctors, but we're not dummies either. If we are going to have even a sliver of a chance of pulling off this miracle, it will all hinge on keeping that foot clean. We can't do that without fresh bandages.

Jeff stabs Henry with one more shot of morphine, leaving us down to our last syringe for the morning. We begin the painstaking process of peeling back the bandages to change them before setting up for the night, and what we find is not good.

"Is that actually turning black?" Jeff asks when he sees the sutures.

"Is it black or is it just dried blood?"

"I'm hoping it's a scab because black would be bad, right? I don't know a whole lot, but I know that much."

"It can't be black from dead skin," I say hopefully. "At least not yet."

"You hope."

Looking at his foot right now I don't expect his toe to make it. How can it? The stitches look okay, I guess. At least they're still holding. But the redness is getting worse, and there's absolutely no feeling in his toe. It's cold to the touch and he can't feel a thing. Like it is dead already.

We'll give it another day and if nothing improves we'll have to reverse the process before the dead tissue starts to rot—that would be a guaranteed infection. Let's hope it doesn't come to that.

The night passes slowly. Jeff and I take turns sitting

up, trying to stay awake. I find that it's a considerably easier task today. Not because I'm so well-rested, but because I'm worrying. I'm worried that Henry's foot will become infected. I'm worried that his toe will need to be cut off (again). I'm worried about Rachael in the village by herself. I'm worried about how we're going to get Henry home. Missionaries aren't supposed to worry, but I'm worried.

These are the sort of things I routinely put in my reports to our supporters back home. I have never been comfortable with how Christians in America portray missionaries as spiritual superheroes. I'm certainly not a spiritual superhero. I'm a guy who struggles with sin, same as everyone else. Right now it's worry. So to stop worrying, I try to pray. I recite every Bible verse I can think of that has to do with being anxious, and it helps a little. Before I know it, it's Jeff's turn to stay up. Or at least I think it is. With no watch, I'm only guessing.

I shake him awake, we check on Henry, and I turn the shotgun over to Jeff. As I settle back against the tree I worry about whether or not I'll be able to sleep, but as I'm apologizing to God for worrying again, and trying to replace it with prayer again, my mind eventually slips into unconsciousness.

## Chapter 9

Sleeping against a tree is not fun. I fidget and turn throughout my nap, trying to get comfortable. When it's over and I open my eyes, I can see the gray light of dawn creeping across the patches of sky exposed between the branches overhead. I flash back to the nights my brother and I would sleep in our treehouse as kids. It wasn't much of a house, because we ran out of wood before we built the roof. But it had four walls, and it was ours. We would sleep out there in the summer, and we always woke up with the dawn.

My reverie doesn't last long but it's enough to momentarily confuse me. The confusion recedes as I start to focus on the scene around me. In the dim light I see the hammock where Henry is sleeping, his right arm dangling out. I see Jeff at the other edge of the clearing, a reading light clipped to the top of his journal. I stretch my legs and the popping of my knees makes Jeff look over. He stands up and we meet in the clearing, our voices hushed to keep from waking Henry. After two days with no coffee, my caffeine headache is in rage mode and I can actually feel my brain pounding against the inside of my skull. I ignore it and concentrate on the conversation with Jeff.

"We need to head back," he says.

"I know. But how?"

"He'll have to ride on one of the bikes. There's no other way."

"I know. But how?"

"I've been thinking, and I remember how my Uncle used to give us rides on the front of his four-wheeler. He would sit on the seat and we would sit on the gas tank. If we draped our feet over the handle bars and he sort of hugged our waist, it would work well enough."

"Isn't he the one you call 'my crazy Uncle Joe'?"

"Well, yeah, but this whole thing has been crazy. We're running out of water and bandages. What choice do we have?"

Theme of the week, apparently.

"It has to be your bike."

"Not that I object, but why does it have to be mine?"

"Because of the gun," I reply.

The shotgun scabbard I rigged up on my dirt bike will prevent anyone from sitting on the gas tank and draping their legs up front. The stock of the gun wouldn't leave any room.

"Okay, I can see that," Jeff says. "But if my arm gets worn out from holding him, we might have to switch."

It's not much of a plan, but it's all we have at the moment. We move quickly and quietly around the camp, picking up what few items we have scattered about. Then we go wake up Henry. Normally we would let him sleep to gain strength and healing, but we have no idea how long the trip back to the village will take and we want to make sure we don't have to spend another night in the jungle.

"How's your foot?" I ask as soon as he's awake.

"Hiveness."

That Kilo word carries an entire phrase's worth of meaning. It means a person isn't doing as well as they would like, but they can't complain because they are doing better than they should be. Ever since I learned it, I have been thinking about its theological implications. Not being okay, but being better than you should be...might be something there.

"Better hiveness than okaa," I reply, using the Kilo word for a downward spiral. I am amazed at the complexity of the Kilo language. There is a dizzying array of variations, every one of them packed with meaning. Simply by changing a prefix inflection, you can convey distinct details or meaning. Needless to say, I'm still learning. If Henry dies, I don't know what it would mean for my studies. Wow, is that a selfish thought, or what?

We explain our plan to Henry, such as it is. He has never ridden one of the motorcycles before and he is skeptical, to say the least.

"I do not like it, but what choice do I have?"

Like I said—theme of the week.

Henry gets out of the hammock with minimal assistance, an improvement over yesterday, and waits while we pack up. Once everything is packed we wheel the bikes over. Jeff gets on and balances the bike, keeping both feet on the ground, while I help Henry balance on one leg. He gingerly lifts his other leg up and half-slides, half-hops onto the gas tank. He leans and scoots while I lift and push, with Jeff fighting to keep the whole sorry thing upright.

We get Henry onto the gas tank, his legs bent at the knee over the handlebars. He can rest his foot on the fender, as long as we don't hit any bumps at high speed. Judging from the angle he's holding his foot, we won't be doing anything at high speed. I'm still holding Henry as Jeff starts the bike. It sputters a bit, the engine soon clears out the cobwebs and smooths out. Jeff wraps his arm around Henry as I climb onto my bike, repeating the start-up procedure. Jeff takes the lead to set the pace and we make our way to the trail.

I wish I had a great story about our "exciting" ride through the jungle. I don't. Mostly what I see as we drive is the rear tire of Jeff's bike. On straight stretches we make decent time, but anything that resembles a corner requires us to slow down considerably. We have to go slow because we can't afford for a branch or bush to snag Henry's toe.

We finally break through a clearing and see the familiar area of the cordaleet. We brake to a stop and kill the motors. They sputter into silence, but almost immediately Henry's head snaps up fast enough to give himself whiplash.

"What on earth? What's…" Jeff says, but is quickly silenced by a raised hand from Henry. No wonder Jeff was startled—Henry's head had come up so quickly that he almost hit Jeff in the nose.

Suddenly, I hear it too.

A short, almost inaudible huff in the brush near us.

"Peebish," Henry whispers.

I don't know that word, but I'm not about to ask right now. That was not a normal jungle sound. It wasn't human either. It was like the snuff/snort that a white-tail buck makes when he senses danger. Part warning, part challenge—every hunter knows that sound means he's been detected.

There are no deer here. No animal with antlers

could survive in the jungle because moving through the densely packed undergrowth would be impossible. I don't know what I heard, but it wasn't a deer.

"Peebish," Henry repeats, softer this time. He lifts his legs down onto the ground.

Slowly, he inches his way to the ground, no hint of pain at all. He is totally focused on the brush to our left, where the snuff/snort came from. I can't believe it—he means to stalk whatever is in there on his hands and knees! He motions that we should stay put, then reaches over and grabs the shotgun. Henry is one of the few Kilo who have fired my gun. I don't know what it is that makes him so different, but he has never been afraid of new things.

He is careful not to bang the barrel against the bike, bringing the gun around quietly and smoothly. He is dead quiet as he creeps forward, no sound at all. His thumb sneaks up and flicks off the gun's safety.

I realize I've stopped breathing, and my heart is thumping so hard I can feel it. I've hunted deer in Michigan, wild pigs in North Carolina, and even elk out in Wyoming, but this is the most edgy I've ever been in the woods. I can feel the tension like a weight on my shoulders. I glance at Jeff and can tell he feels the same way.

Then the image of a jaguar leaps into my mind, and I am no longer just tense. Now I'm terrified. Jeff has the same thought at the same time and his eyes go big and bug out, like in a cartoon. I'm amazed that I could think about cartoons right now, but that's what he looks like.

I look back at Henry just in time to see him raise

the shotgun, and the world shifts into slow motion. I see the flexing of muscles in his forearm. I see his finger tighten on the trigger. He pulls it, and I brace for what's coming. I flinch when I see the tug of his finger and then…

Nothing.

No shot. No noise. Henry looks a question at me, wondering why the gun didn't work. A light bulb goes off in my head and I remember: the gun is loaded, but there is no shell in the chamber, only in the magazine.

I silently pantomime the motions for loading a shell, trying not to make a sound. He seems to understand, but there's a new problem: racking a shotgun is not quiet. He will have to move quickly to get the gun pumped, back on his shoulder, and fired, before the jaguar pounces from the brush.

God help us, we need another miracle.

I'm still holding my breath and my lungs are burning. My heart stops as Henry jerks into motion. He swings the gun down and wrenches his forearms to rack the slide. He rotates his body back into firing position before his brain registers that nothing on the gun moved.

There's a crashing sound in the bush and I cry out as I fight to keep my eyes open. My brain registers three separate but simultaneous thoughts:

1) *The action release!* There's a little nub next to the trigger that has to be pressed for the slide to work. It's a safety feature. The gun didn't load because Henry forgot about it in the heat of the moment.

2) *We're gonna die!* A jaguar is pouncing and we're history.

3) *Wait…that sound is* going away *from us*.

My body swings into motion, reaching for the gun. Then thought number three hits my brain and I realize I'm not gonna die. In fact, I can barely even hear the crashing anymore.

I stop, my arm outstretched toward Henry, my mind awash in confusion. I don't have conscious thoughts, only a few semi-coherent emotions. I'm ecstatic at not being mauled by a jaguar. I'm confused as to why it ran. I'm trembling from the adrenaline coursing through my body.

Henry hasn't moved. He is simply staring into the brush. He must be in shock.

Jeff breaks the silence.

"What was that? A jaguar? How did…"

"No jaguar," Henry says.

His body deflates as the wind goes out of him with the words. He is instantly in pain as his mind returns to normal.

"What then?"

"Wapa," Henry says, whispering.

"Wapa?" I ask, jumping in. "How do you know?"

"I hear," Henry says quietly, his voice barely a whisper. "No other animal sounds like that."

"Did you see it? How can you be sure?"

"Jaguars do not run." Henry says. "It was Wapa."

I roll a stump over for Henry to put his foot on, then go to refuel the bikes. They both need gas, but Jeff's bike is running on fumes. Peering into the tank I can actually see the bottom and it looks dry. Amazing that we made it this far—there can't be much left in the lines.

Looking at the level of each tank, Jeff asks what we're both thinking.

"We gonna make it?"

"I think so."

"You hope so."

"Yeah."

"One way to find out," he says. "Plus, what…"

"Have we got to lose?" I finish for him.

We push the bikes to where Henry is. He struggles to his feet. If it was me missing a toe, I'd be down for the count and you'd need a stretcher to carry me home. Okay, maybe I wouldn't be that bad, but I wouldn't be riding on a trail and facing off with a big animal like Henry has been.

"I must get back," he says. "I must warn them."

"Warn them?" I ask.

"The Wapa. He will be there soon enough."

I start to say something else but I don't finish. I'm not convinced it was a Wapa that almost attacked us, but I decide not to push it. Besides, I'm in a hurry to get home too. Two nights of sleeping next to a tree plus all this trail riding have me looking forward to my bed.

The rest of the ride back is uneventful, just slow. Jeff and I switch bikes and I take the lead. The routine is the same, but the going is easier. With a wider trail, we keep a faster pace. It still takes most of the day. We drink the last of the water about halfway there, using the last morphine shot for Henry. He needed it.

We round some familiar bends and I can see the opening in the trees ahead that signals the airstrip. My back aches. My legs are burning. I can't feel my hands.

I'm not about to complain though, not with Henry perched on the gas tank in front of me. His feet are dangling, still awkwardly resting on the fender. He is incredible. I don't know how he does it. I'm sure he is feeling the pain, but it doesn't show. A life of jungle living has built his muscles and hardened his body in a way no gym ever could.

When we finally reach the edge of the village, we can tell right away that something big is happening there. A crowd has gathered around a bonfire in the growing twilight, and the Kilo are ringing the fire in a way that reminds me of Indian rain dances. My eyes search the crowd and I spot the girls off to the side, part of the group, but not really. They look like wall-flowers at a dance, standing by themselves.

Soon enough someone notices us. Deedap comes running over. His smile is so wide it threatens to split his face.

"Father! I am so happy you are here!"

At least that's what I think he says. He is speaking Kilo so fast I can't understand it all. Henry and Deedap have a frenzied reunion, words flying back and forth like tennis balls during warmups at Wimbledon. When their excitement wanes somewhat, Deedap turns to me and we shake in the traditional Kilo manner. He surprises me by speaking in perfect English.

"Thank you. You served us well."

Unbelievably, his smile actually brightens even more. He is beaming bright enough to light up a Christmas tree. I smile back, both in relief at being home and in joy over his English. He has obviously been practicing and I'm touched by his enthusiasm.

"Blobershtish," I reply. Essentially, "You're welcome, it was my pleasure."

Turning to Henry, Deedap announces, "Come, Father. And see."

He turns and we all follow, walking toward the far side of the circle. As our eyes adjust to the light from the fire, we see a dark shape lying on the ground near it. Children are looking warily from behind their mothers while teenagers gaze openly. Several spears protrude from the large object. We approach slowly, since Henry is now leaning on Deedap like a crutch. It's an animal, but not like anything I've seen here before.

Stopping a yard short, we look down as Deedap beams up at us. It looks like a bear, but it can't be a bear. Bears don't live here. But that's the only thing I can compare it to. It has dirty black fur, gray in some areas. It has large paws and small ears, pointed just a bit. They look too small for the body, which is larger than most of the black bears we have back home in Michigan, but smaller than a Grizzly.

What gets me most is the face. It looks like someone took the normal face of a bear and smooshed it in. Smears of white give it a raccoon-like look. When I think of bears I think of big teeth, long noses, and large faces. But this thing has none of that. It has a small jaw, a short snout, and a pinched face.

"Peebish," Henry says quietly. It's the same thing I heard him whisper earlier.

"What does that mean?" I ask. "And what is this?"

"*Peebish* means 'May it be so,'" he whispers. "And that, Mister Neighbor, is a Wapa."

"How do you know?" I ask. "It looks like…"

I almost said "looks like a smooshed bear to me," but I think better of it and stop in mid-sentence. Sometimes the better part of Tribal Missions is knowing when to keep your mouth shut. I simply squeeze Henry's shoulder, take in the look of satisfaction and wonder on his face, and turn to go. I leave him there and go to find my wife. And coffee. It may be almost bedtime, but I don't even care. I want to hug my wife and I want some coffee.

I have a momentary pang of conscience that says now would be a great time to kick the habit. I've gone two days without it and I know if I can stick it out for another 24 hours I could probably break my addiction completely. It's only a fleeting thought and I pause long enough to let it pass before I head for home. I can quit anytime I want, but that time is not now!

## Chapter 10

A month has now passed since that fateful night. The Kilo spent most of it celebrating. The Wapa was skinned and roasted, with everyone partaking at some point. The kids each received only a small portion, but everyone had some. The hide was hoisted aloft like a trophy, sometimes even passed overhead from group to group like a crowd surfer at a concert. At one point Rachael and I stood on the front porch holding hands and observing from a distance. The elders took turns wearing the skin like a cape, dancing around the fire, just like the old American Indians.

The hunting party had arrived shortly after we did, having followed the trail of the Wapa in a circle back toward the cordaleet and eventually to the village. So Henry truly did hear and smell the Wapa in the brush that day, and our encounter with it drove the big beast back toward the village, just ahead of us and the frustrated hunting group.

So, ironically, it wasn't any of the experienced Kilo hunters or the Indiana Jones-type missionaries who killed the Wapa. Kanteel, the teenage boy sent back to the village earlier, and several of the women kept their wits about them and armed themselves after the Wapa burst through the brush and started pacing menacingly in the Commons. Kanteel rushed it with an axe in an incredibly brave (or stupid?) act that will make him a hero in the tribe for the rest of his life, but he actually wouldn't have succeeded without the women who speared the counter-attacking animal. When I heard about all this I was reminded of the Bible story about the young David killing a bear and a lion. It also renewed my ongoing appreciation for the strength of the Kilo women—they also stand as village heroes, and rightly so.

Miraculously, no one was injured before the raging Wapa collapsed and died. From what I learned about it later, Kanteel's attack may have actually been a smart thing to do, because these partly carnivorous animals have been known to kill and eat creatures as large as horses and cattle. Considering that the Wapa was on the run, far from its natural territory, and probably hungry, who knows what it might have done to some of the villagers, especially the children.

The Wapa turned out to be an Andean Short-Faced Bear, or "Spectacled Bear" as it's also known. After things settled down a bit Rachael and I looked it up in our printed copy of *Indigenous South American Jungle Animals* (until we finally get that satellite internet connection, we'll keep learning things the old-fashioned way). The bears are listed as a "vulnerable" species, and hunting them is illegal. This concerns me somewhat, as I am unsure about how that might affect the Kilo. The relationship of indigenous tribes to the government is always a bit complicated, especially as it relates to conservation and the environment. But that seems more like a theoretical problem than a real one at this point. I have no idea when a government official last visited the Kilo, but it hasn't been anytime recently.

Henry's foot healed fine, looking remarkably healthy only a week or so after we returned to the village. We didn't have any more morphine to give him, but he got by with the ibuprofen we had in our house. Like I said, he's one tough guy.

His toe was another matter, however. It looked like we had run out of miracles. The redness and inflammation went away, which was good, but the gray/black had replaced it. We worried incessantly about infection from dead tissue. We showed Henry's wife how to change the dressing but still insisted he come by the house so we could evaluate the healing process. We were about to cut our losses and re-remove his toe.

And then, unwrapping the bandage one day, Rachael gasped and clasped her hand to her mouth.

"What?" I asked. "Is it that bad?"

"Not at all—look!"

I did take a look, and almost couldn't believe what I saw. There was color in his toe. The gray skin surrounding the sutures was trending back to normal, almost matching the rest of his leg. He still had no feeling, but at least there were signs of blood flow.

We kept a close watch over Henry every day after that, but things only got better. His toe regained its full color and he recovered some feeling and movement. Now, a month later, he's almost back to normal. In the last week or so he has even recovered well enough to resume his dictation work with me. Our worst fears— that Henry would die, we would lose our friend, and the Kilo Bible translation would be derailed—have not materialized after all. My first surgery turned out to be a success, though I'm still not eager to try another one any time soon.

The man who cut Henry still gets teased about it (they call him Toe Cutter), and Henry doesn't have full range of motion in his foot and toe. But all-in-all, that's nothing compared to how bad it might have been.

Right now I'm sitting at my computer, trying to compose an update for our supporters back home. Our Prayer Profile is a week overdue and I've been procrastinating. How am I supposed to tell this story? How can I convey the roller coaster ride we've been on this week in just a page or two?

Jungle camping, midnight rides, improvised surgery, and a hunt for a near-mythical animal have all got to fit in here somehow, because they're all missionary storytelling gold. I want to make the most of it, I'm just not sure how. Maybe I'll end up writing it all down, I don't know. But one thing I do know right now is this: I'm changing the heading at the top of the page.

Crossing out the word *Tribal*, I type in my new heading, a designation I plan to milk for all it's worth.

Ian and Rachael Allen:
*Jungle* Missionaries to the Kilo People

## Acknowledgments

Writing a book is largely an exercise in solitude. Bringing it to print is not. Sincere thanks go to each of the following people for their essential contributions in the making of this book: To my wife Natalie, for perceiving before anyone else that a novel about Tribal Missions could be a reality and for giving me the encouragement to make it so. To Noah Bowman, for creating the Kilo language using only the brain things inside of his head. To the Frieling family: Jason, Kristin, Katelyn, and Megan, for being the first people to actually read the manuscript and giving the idea the life it needed. To Dave Swavely, for believing in the project and for helping me to see that what makes sense to me in my head does not always make sense to a reader on the page. To the missionaries at every level of Ethnos360: you formed much of my motivation and inspiration for writing and you are gospel heroes. And finally, to you, the reader. Thank you for reading and for getting to know Ian. Now "go thou and do likewise," until the whole word hears! I am always glad to hear from readers and I promise to respond back if you want to contact me. You can reach me at:

erniebowmanauthor@gmail.com

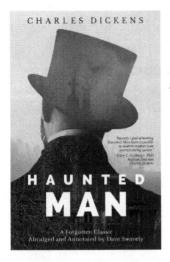

# HAUNTED MAN

*by Charles Dickens* | *140 pages*

*A Forgotten Classic*

*Abridged and Annotated by Dave Swavely*

*bit.ly/hauntedman*

A college professor named Redlaw is a good man plagued by bad memories of a traumatic childhood, compounded by a terrible betrayal and loss during his young adulthood. When an ethereal demonic doppelganger of himself appears and offers to wipe away those memories, Redlaw eagerly accepts, and also receives the ability to spread this "gift" to others.

Featuring the breathless suspense, colorful characters, and witty humor that has made Dickens such a beloved author, the story also tackles some of the deepest philosophical and theological questions ever raised in his writings. His answer to "the problem of evil" is of both literary and religious interest.

*"Swavely's goal of making Haunted Man more accessible to modern readers is an overwhelming success."*
  **–Dr. Gary L. Colledge** (*PhD, University of St. Andrews, author of* God and Charles Dickens

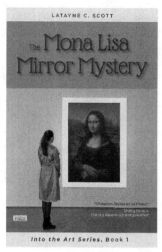

## THE MONA LISA MIRROR MYSTERY

*Into the Art Series, Book 1*
*by Latayne C. Scott | 108 pages*

Night at the Museum *meets*
A Wrinkle in Time*!*

*bit.ly/Mona-Lisa-Mirror*

Addy's three friends don't know what to think when Addy tells them she "whooshed" right back into time and met a quirky Leonardo daVinci. Is it a dream? And what do the girls do when they have just as much drama in the present?

"Christian fiction at its finest!" –**Shelly Beach**, Christy Award-winning author

"Crosses space and time…The Mona Lisa Mirror Mystery is for the lover of mysteries and art." –**Patti Hill**, author, *The San Clemente Bait Shop*; *Telephony*

"A book your teen won't want to miss. . .I will recommend it over and over." –**Celeste Green**, Academic Dean, Oak Grove Classical Academy

"So imaginative, so engaging. Well done." –**Sharon K. Souza,** author, *What We Don't Know*

"The characters are well developed and the plot has a way of drawing you directly into the action. I can't wait to read the next one." –**Joy Capps**, HomeSchoolLiterature.com